About the author

Born in Hammersmith, West London, but I moved to Clacton-on-Sea in Essex where I was raised. I am now settled in Ipswich, Suffolk with my husband, James, our Tabby cat, Tabitha, and son, Hudson, our little miracle baby boy who is the greatest of all my achievements. I have a very close and supportive mum, dad, sister and two brothers.

12 MONTHS TO ' I DO '

Victoria Fenn

12 MONTHS TO ' I DO '

Vanguard Press

A CIP catalogue record for this title is
available from the British Library.

ISBN 978-1-80016-050-7

Vanguard Press is an imprint of
Pegasus Elliot MacKenzie Publishers Ltd.
www.pegasuspublishers.com

First Published in 2021

Vanguard Press
Sheraton House Castle Park
Cambridge England

Printed & Bound in Great Britain

Dedication

For all abused children, it was not your fault.

Love

I have had boyfriends in the past, but no one has made me feel like Edward James. I knew from the first time I actually had a proper conversation with him he was the one, cheesy as it sounds. But when you know you just know, and if you have not had that feeling yet you obviously haven't met that special someone. The sort of person that makes you a better version of yourself, makes you see yourself in a different light, encourages your dreams and is by your side through everything. Real love.

I think back to the first time I felt love for someone other than my family. I was eleven, he was thirteen. I lived on a road in a small town by the sea where all the kids from neighbouring houses played out the front after school and at the weekend. It was safe back then and the roads were quiet, so our parents weren't concerned about us getting run over or being kidnapped; we just got left to it.

There was a playing field near our three-bed semi where we would play until it got dark with water balloons and water guns, playing IT and hide and seek. That's what we did for fun. We did have basic computer games, but why play with them when we could be outside in the fresh air? Weather seemed to be better back then, too. We used to have a summer that seemed to last for weeks rather than days. Mobile phones were non-existent. You must be thinking I am ancient, but I was born in the eighties. Your friends had to knock for you or call the land line, as that's all there was back then. Not like nowadays when you can text so easily. These were the sorts of times where if you wanted a question answered you couldn't just look online on your phone. You had to either go the library and get a book on it, or use dial up internet which seemed to take forever to connect. You couldn't just download a film, or a box set on the TV, either. You had to wait until it was released from the cinema unless you bought a dodgy pirate copy, or wait until it was available to rent or buy from the video store or video man that used to come round once a week. These were different times to what we are living through right now. Technology has come on so much in the last few years, it's scary to think that if I have children what life will be like for them growing up in a generation where social media is already taking over, and nothing is private any more. It's like living in a world where your mobile phone is a spy and listens and remembers anything you say or look up on the internet.

There was this one boy. He went to a different school to me, but he lived on the same road. He was cool, tall and good looking and his name was Spence Egerton. All the girls fancied him, might have had something to do with his curtained blonde hair, blue eyes and chiselled features, but he wouldn't look twice at me, because 1.) I was two years younger and 2.) I was short, kind of dumpy, had dark features and boring brown hair and was spotty. I had a strange sense of dressing for a child too. For some reason I loved a pair of black trousers and would pair this with a suit jacket. Yes, you heard right. I was an eleven-year-old girl who liked to dress smartly in a suit. I was not popular and didn't have golden hair like the girls the boys seemed to fancy at school.

But he was friendly and nice to me, even came to birthday parties for my younger siblings. The moment I knew it was love was when one day he stood up for me. There was another boy who lived around the corner who would always make fun of me. Push me off of my bike when I would ride past him. He was a little shit, to be polite. I kind of got used to him bullying me, but one day he actually spat at me when I walked past him, Spence saw what happened ran over and immediately lifted the boy up by his throat and said if he ever did that again or did anything to upset me in the future, he would be coming after him. I never knew threatening behaviour could be so attractive, I fell in love there and then I was hooked. I had it bad, I would walk past his house most days hoping to get a glimpse of him. His bedroom was at the front and he would always have his window open whatever the weather belting out the same song over and over. This is, and always has been, my favourite song ever since I first heard him play it.

Nothing ever really happened between me and Spence even though I longed and dreamed about it for years.

He is now happily married. We are still in contact but don't get to see each other that often any more. It's hard to make time for each other when you're in a relationship, work full time, have a house, but I knew if I needed him, he would be there. We have both seen each other through heartache, break ups and deaths in the family. He has always had an opinion on my relationships and my bad habits; smoking was one of them. I have been smoke free now for three years, other than the odd occasional drunken slip up so he couldn't moan at me about that any more. But we were similar, I guess. I nagged him too, about his partying ways, but it was only because I wanted the best for him. I did try and set him up with a few girls over the years hoping he would say it was me he wanted before he met Sarah, but he never seemed interested in anyone. He seemed extremely picky. There was a point in time during our clubbing days where we had a drunken moment and almost kissed and, for a second, I thought maybe we could be something more and maybe, just maybe, he felt the same as me.

That night was one of those random unplanned nights that were always the best it was only supposed to be a quiet couple of drinks with my sister but ended up into an all-night bender. We ended up in the one and only nightclub in town the only place open past twelve other than the kebab shops and we bumped into him not long before closing. He was clearly pissed as he was dancing and when I walked in his face lit up like he hadn't seen me for years. I couldn't help smiling as at that moment I felt beautiful something I had not felt since the abuse. My tummy was doing somersaults and definitely had a flutter in my lady parts I often felt this when I was around him. No one else had ever made me feel like this until I met Edward. He pulled me into one of the grotty burgundy velour covered booths that surrounded the dance floor usually the place you would go for a grope or a snog towards the end of the night or the place to leave your drunk friend looking after coats and bags while you enjoyed your night. He looked right into my eyes and said, "I really wish I could kiss you right now."

If I had the confidence, I would have grabbed his face and rammed my tongue down his throat as I had always imagined doing ever since I was eleven. But I brushed it off, even laughed at him and told him don't be so silly. I can still picture his piercing blue eyes staring into mine. I wanted to tell him so much how I felt but something held me back, I was scared of ruining our friendship when to him it may have just been a one-off drunken kiss as he had, had a skinful. I always think about that night and wonder what would have happened if we did kiss? I spoke to my sister about it in the way home and she said I should have just kissed him. What did I have to lose? Would we be together now, would it be us that was married? We never spoke about it; I don't know if he remembered he had even said it and not long after that he met his wife.

I remember the first time he introduced me to Sarah. Mrs perfect, I thought, straight away. I was instantly jealous. When he called me not long after they had been together and told me he had proposed, I wanted to be sick. I felt like my heart was going to break. It was lucky he told me over the phone as he would have known by my facial expression and the tears that instantly fell from my eyes that I wasn't exactly thrilled. That was it. I could never tell him how I felt now It was too late. It was so hard at the time I couldn't look at any posts he put on social media of them together and I had to pretend to be interested when he would call me, to let me know of the latest wedding plans, when inside I was crying. The hardest thing was seeing him at the altar. I had dreamt about this in my youth, but in the dream, I was the bride. It was then the realisation hit that nothing other than friendship was going to happen between us. I went off the rails a bit during that time, going out and getting pissed Thursday, Friday and Saturday nights, sleeping with any men that would pay me attention, regardless of what they were like. I had sex with more men during that few months than I had in my entire life. Sex was meaningless to me before Edward I didn't enjoy it would just do it because that is what the bloke wanted they could do whatever they wanted to me and I would just lay there like a ghost. As he said his vows, I was waiting for him to shout over to me and say India it's you I want to marry instead of Sarah, but sadly he didn't. I got very emotional when they were pronounced man and wife. Not happy tears at all. I wanted someone to look at me the way Spence looked at Sarah with so much love in his eyes. I wanted that, I deserved that, didn't I, to be loved.

The rest of the wedding was a bit of a blur I just ended up drinking most of the free wine on the table during the wedding breakfast, white, rosé, red—it was all the same to me—and I ended up waking up next to the best man, naked.

Shagging the best man not one of my finest moments and to this day Spence does not know what happened I did not need his judgement. I think he just thought I got drunk and passed out. Little did he know that I had to sneak out of his best man's room, wearing only his suit jacket, and do the walk of shame back to the room I was staying in. Luckily, no one saw me. Well, I hope they didn't anyway.

I had never thought that I would get married only in my dreams when I was younger. Who would want to marry me? I was damaged goods. I had always had issues with how I see myself. People could tell me a million times that I am beautiful, but I would just go back to the abuse and the names I was called at school for having olive skin or being fat and ugly. My nickname at school was broomstick, due to resembling a witch. I can remember when I left junior school everyone wrote on my school top with messages of good luck, most people would keep there's as a keepsake but I chucked mine in the bin as it had broomstick written all over it. No one would call me by my actual name, India Halberd.

I was rummaging through my bedside table drawer looking for my credit card I kept in there for emergencies, this was an emergency as I had wedding bits to buy. I knew it was in there, why is it when you are trying to look for something you can never find it? Pushing old receipts, buttons and other crap I kept for no reason at all out of the way, a photo of my younger self appeared. I smiled, something I only seemed to do now when Edward was around. It took me back to a time I felt so confident and carefree. Wearing my dark hair super straight so long it went down to my bum, tanned skin and brown almond shaped eyes. Eleven years old and dressed in a designer white shirt with red tartan waistcoat and matching trousers. My mum always treated me to the best things; she always had for as long as I could remember. This picture was taken at a time when I loved being the centre of attention, would push my siblings out of photographs as I wanted it to just be all about me. The men in my life had slowly taken my confidence away bit by bit day by day.

If you were to glance at me, you may think I am younger than I am, not because I am very youthful, but because I am still very short, a tad on the curvaceous side, some days you could say fat and look pregnant even though I'm nowhere near. I blame the endometriosis for the fat part. When I was thirty, I started to experience pelvic pain and my tummy would swell up so much I could only wear elasticated clothing. Very attractive, I know. Sometimes it would be so bad I couldn't get out of bed. It wasn't until after persistently pestering the doctors I saw a specialist who gave me exploratory surgery and I was diagnosed. I knew it wasn't period pain like they thought. It's a common condition that currently affects one in ten women and it is where your womb lining grows in other places. In a way I was relieved, as I was starting to think maybe it was all in my head. This surgery did not solve my pain. It will still flare up at any time not just around my period and was so unpredictable.

Comparing myself now to the photo, my skin is still tanned but freckled from the sun, fine lines and dark circles around the eyes. Crooked teeth that I had always hated but there I was smiling flashing my straight white teeth in the picture.

The only time I would do this now would be on a night out if I was drunk, because then I didn't care until the pictures would emerge on social media in the morning. I hated myself, had no confidence like I use to, I think that's probably why I have never settled down before never felt good enough that's why I never told Spence how I truly felt about him. I wasn't going to make that same mistake with Edward, let my past affect my future. I never wear much make up unless it's a special occasion or have a spot that's needs covering up. I wear more make up then as a distraction, so you don't directly look at the massive red flashing bump on my face. I do not live for fashion. I do buy clothes that are in fashion, but only if I like them. You would not catch me in a pair of tie dye cycling shorts and sporting a bum bag just because it was in fashion, because if you ask me it's bloody gross. If I were to describe my style in two words, it would be 'granny chic'.

I have always been the sensible one. I have never had a girlie holiday but, if I did, and we all got tacky tee-shirts made up, mine would probably say 'the sensible one' or 'I'll have a coffee and then I'll get on it.' This used to be my catchphrase from past nights out on the town. Bet you wish you had a friend like me, hey. Well, it has some advantages as I would make sure you kept hydrated with lots of water, pretend I am buying you a vodka and coke but actually just buy you a coke. I would make sure you got home, and even on some occasions undress you and put you to bed. Thinking about it, I should hire out my services. I am the only person who would ask for a hot drink in a nightclub. You can imagine the confused looks I would get from bar staff wondering if there was something wrong with me or thinking they had misheard, but unfortunately that is just me. There have been more than a few times when I have let loose, got drunk, even danced, especially after Spence's wedding and during my time at uni but I am so much better looking after people than them looking after me. I was lucky to not get an STD or not get killed during that time as I didn't know the blokes I would be going home with. That's probably why I am most suited to my job.

I work full time as a nurse at a local hospital and although it is bloody hard work, I love it, I started out as a healthcare assistant and on my first day someone died whilst I was washing them. The other members of staff on shift that day knew that it was only a matter of time, but they didn't tell me that. Surprisingly, I went back, and death was a daily occurrence on the ward I was on due to the age of the patients. It was like the ward they were sent to die—horrible, I know—so I got kind of numb to it in the end. The good thing was you didn't get time to form a connection with anyone so it didn't upset me, that was life, I can't complain as this is where I met Edward, when I was taking Mrs. Jackson with her dodgy hip for an X-ray, as he was a radiographer. If it wasn't for this job, I would not have met him. It put things into perspective too, being on a ward surrounded by death made me think that life was really too short and I felt like I had wasted most of mine being wrapped in my past and just wanting to disappear. So, I took the leap and moved away from my hometown, family and friends by the seaside in Essex to be with him in Suffolk.

It did make sense too with the commute as I was travelling to the hospital there every day anyway. We had no children yet. This could be an issue if we did decide to have kids because of my endometriosis. I always thought something could be wrong as I hadn't fallen pregnant by accident and I hadn't exactly been careful if you know what I mean over the years. Edward was aware of this he has been by my side from my diagnosis and knew that this could be a possibility and still proposed. I suppose we were pretty 'normal' not that I like using that word, really. Not rich or poor, somewhere in between.

Anyway, you probably have a good picture of me in your head now. Sorry, peeps, this is what I go through every day when I look in the mirror. But guess what, I have a year to change things; not cosmetic things, but how I feel about myself inside. I may even try to grow my bobbed hair out. I have had the same haircut since I was thirteen. The only difference would be sometimes I would have a fringe cut in and other times I would grow it out. But Edward wants to marry me, so I can't be that bad, can I? I just need to start believing it, but it's hard with everything that has happened to me in the past. Anyway, this is my twelve-month journey until the big day.

September

It's a year to go, oh my god how scary. Looking outside into my long and skinny garden from upstairs in my two up, two down, terraced house, I was hoping it would rain today, purely because my logic was that if it rained today it is more likely to be sunny next year. But you guessed it, actual blue skies, birds singing, trees gently swaying in the breeze. Not too hot, not to cold, perfect wedding weather, oh shit. Well, if it rains it rains, what is the worst that can happen? I can just picture now my caked-on makeup being washed off by torrential downpours and my eyes looking like a panda, much the same as I look after showering when I do wear make-up. That is the only problem with planning a wedding: there is one thing you have no control over; even if you get married in summer you cannot guarantee the weather these days. Unless you get married in a country that is always hot, but knowing my luck it would still chuck it down. It would be a freak storm or something like nothing seen for a hundred years. I cannot believe it's a year away today, it is going to fly by, like the last six months has.

My issues with myself had started as a child. When I was eleven, I met Malcolm. He had started renovating a house he bought on the same road as me. A lot of the kids would do odd jobs for him and so did Spence. I can remember the first time I went there. I was excited as I approached the newly painted red door with Spence by my side. Malcolm let us in and welcomed us with a smile which made me feel at ease straight away. The smell of paint hit me as soon as I crossed the threshold and the bare floorboards creaked with every step I took; this place needed a lot of work.

There was barely any furniture, just one or two items in each room, old, antique looking and dusty. In the kitchen there was one cupboard with a worktop, so the kettle had a place to sit, which was covered in grubby finger marks all over the outside. I think it was originally white. A couple of tea-stained mugs and an opened pint of green milk with a teaspoon just lying on the sugar littered worktop.

I hoped he did not offer me a cup of tea because I would have accepted as it wasn't polite to say no, I made sure I would bring my own drink if I ever came back. I thought how overdressed I was in my black high waisted trousers and floaty blouse, not the sort of clothes for cleaning. But my clothes were all this sort of style so I didn't really have anything more causal. Spence had taken the mickey out of me as per usual when he saw me, saying I looked like I was going to a wedding or christening or something as I could not possibly be going to do work in those clothes. Spence always took the piss out of the way I dressed and he nicknamed me Posh after one of the biggest girl group members at the time. I did not even own a pair of jeans and luckily, I was the oldest of four so I did not have to wear any hand-me-downs. Unlucky or lucky for my sister, she would get all my old suit jackets and trousers that didn't fit me no more, poor girl. My mum was always buying me new things; I was very spoilt, didn't know how she afforded it really. Being a single mum, probably all on tick from the catalogue. She had brought us up on her own since I was seven. We would see our dad, but only at the weekends if his new wife would let him. He married a horrible woman who really was an evil step mum, as cliché as it sounds, but she hated us, I am sure of it, especially me. She just wanted him to pay all the attention to her daughter, Debbie. I must admit, I was jealous when they would go on family days out without us, more so because my brothers and sister were missing out. I can remember the night so clearly that the family split up. I overheard a conversation where my dad asked my mum if she was having an affair. I didn't know what an affair was, but I knew it couldn't have been a good thing as after that night he moved out.

For weeks after he left, I use to steal my mum's cassette tapes of love songs and play them on my Walkman and cry myself to sleep. If I hear one of those songs now on the radio it takes me straight back to my bedroom that I shared with my younger sister, when I would cry quietly into my pillow so I did not wake her.

That day I swept away debris from the dusty floorboards at Malcolm's and scraped paint off the windowpanes, and had a laugh with Spence who had to leave a bit earlier than me as he had a football match that evening. I felt comfortable enough to stay and finish up on my own otherwise I would have left with him. Black was not a good colour to wear as it showed up every dirty mark, but it would be impossible to stay clean anyway, as you walked up against dusty things without even realising it. I was not into sport at all as I did not want to have to wear trainers, I did not even own a pair. I had to wear plimsolls at school for PE when I did not forge a letter from my mum and that was bad enough, but I drew the line at any kind of sports attire. I was finishing up and about to leave when Malcolm hugged me. It took me a bit by surprise, and it was a hug that lasted longer than my nana's hugs, and they were long.

I just thought he was happy with my work. He then gave me a quid and said he hoped he would see me again. You may think a quid totally not worth it, but to an eleven-year-old in 1997, it was not bad.

Walking home, I kept thinking about the hug and how strange it was, and how I could still smell him on me. He seemed like a nice man, everyone thought so. He'd even been around my mum's house a few times for coffee, but she didn't call him Malcolm. They acted like they had known each other for years as he called my mum Mar, when her name was Marie, which was strange. When I first heard him say it, I thought he was calling her mum. I thought, bloody hell, have I got an extremely older brother that you haven't told me about, as he was well old, I would have said older than my mum, so that would not have been possible.

Maybe he was just one of those huggy people. You know, like the ones that must hug you every time they see you? My mum was one of those. So, I just shrugged it off. If only I knew what was coming.

Men

As cheesy as it sounds, I am going to marry the man of my dreams, and nightmares, lol, if you see his zombie impression. He is tall, well built, handsome, fair very short hair, eyes so blue that I could tell the colour of them from the other side of the room. He used to have longish hair when we first met, but that all changed after I offered to cut his hair one evening. This was early on in our relationship in 2014, when all you do is try to please the other person and basically let them do what they want, so he thought, what's the worst that could happen. I had done a bit of hairdressing when I left school, but I did not like the actual cutting people's hair part, so decided probably not the best profession for me. I was just so worried about fucking someone's hair up. But I still had a bit of knowledge on how to do a quick trim up at least. I did go to hairdressing college one day a week for at least two months. Needless to say, things didn't quite go to plan. I ended up cutting an m sized shape onto the back of Edwards head, don't ask me how I did it. But the only way of salvaging it was to clipper all his hair off, a number two all over, and he has kept it short ever since. He always jokes that I am the reason he has no hair. I don't know if he realizes that he could grow it back again.

I could never understand why he would be interested in me, I still don't, we are very mismatched, but I was lucky: not only was he beautiful to look at, I could be myself, and a version of me I never knew was there. He knew everything that had happened to me when I was younger with Malcolm. Just not a detailed version, some things he didn't need to know. I wish I didn't know. Spence was the only other person who knew what happened to me. But no one knew about the others.

Men had always seemed to be the issue ever since I was a little girl. I felt I was not only attractive to paedophiles, I actually thought that there was an invisible sign on my head that only they could see saying easy target, eager to please. I had always been drawn to the wrong ones; the only right one before Edward was Spence but he wasn't interested in me in that sort of way.

It had all started when my so called 'Uncle M' sat my then seven-year-old self on his lap and shouted to my mum in the kitchen.

"She's going to be a heartbreaker when she's older," he said, kissing me on the lips, holding his hands over my ears, pulling me closer so I could not escape. This only happened when my mum was not around. The thought of those sloppy wet kisses now made me feel physically sick. His breath smelling of coffee and fags still haunted me.

At first, I enjoyed going to Malcolm's as I would see Spence, but then he would start splitting us up, making me work upstairs and him downstairs or vice versa, and that's when it wasn't a cuddle any more, that was the problem.

I told Spence everything that Malcolm had been doing to me when he came round to my house one summer evening. I can remember that night like it was yesterday as it was the last time, I stepped foot in that house. It was a warm night and I was sweating from the humidity when I left Malcolm's. I walked the streets for a while, the smell of charcoal in the air from evening barbecues. When I arrived home, he was there. I can remember my mum giggling as I opened the back door and the theme tune for a popular gameshow, which had come out earlier that year, was on the TV. You would have thought that my mum was the thirteen-year-old, not me, at the time.

I took a deep breath, painted on a smile and wiped my face dry with the cuffs of my blazer from the tears. I tried to sneak past quietly without my mum seeing, but no such luck.

"India, is that you? Look who's popped round." I knew who it was even before I saw his face as the scent of his aftershave filled the house.

Malcolm was a similar age to my mum, early forties, not her usual type at all. She would usually go for twenty-year olds.

I poked my head round the living room door. "Yes, Mum, it's me!" Who else would it be, I thought unless you have let my younger brothers and sister roam the streets at night.

"You look awful, love."

My face was ashen. I am not surprised I looked awful. I was not expecting to see Malcolm sitting on our sofa. Especially after what had just happened.

"You okay?"

No, I was not okay, but I lied. I was getting good at lying now. I use to lie to my dad when I was younger when mum would take me to see my 'Uncle M.' I didn't mind though at the time as I was a child and would be bribed with sweets and ice cream.

"Yeah, just feeling a bit sick, that's all," I replied as I kissed my mum on the cheek. Feeling sick was an understatement. I avoided Malcolm's stare, but I could feel his eyes following me as I hurried up the stairs.

I felt like I could not breathe. As soon as I got in my room I locked the door. New clothing bags covered my bed again. Twice that week I had gone home to bags of new clothing.

I felt so dirty, like I was covered in germs, did not want to touch anything in my room just in case I contaminated anything until I had stripped off and showered. As the warm water hit my face, the tears started to fall again. I had scrubbed my body like it was diseased, until it was red and sore and hurt like it did on the inside. I looked at my naked body in the misted mirror and felt disgusted and fell to the floor sobbing.

I stuffed my dirty clothes, smelling of the same aftershave that filled the air downstairs, in the back of my wardrobe and hid my knickers stained with blood under the bed. I pushed all the bags to the floor and just laid there staring up at the ceiling, focusing on the white brush marks from the paint that I had never noticed before. A knock on the front door made me jump. Who was that at this time of night, I thought, looking at the clock. But it was only seven p.m. It just seemed a lot later; it had been a hell of a day, after all.

'India, India,' Mum called up the stairs. 'Spence is here to see you.'

I didn't move, just continued laying on my bed. I felt numb. I didn't want Spence to see me in this state but it was too late, he was already at my bedroom door. Bloody Mother, I thought, letting him up the stairs.

'Let me in' he said banging on the door.

I quickly let him in as I did not want to arouse suspicion as Mum might have caught on that something was wrong.

'What the fuck happened to you?' he said as soon as he saw me.

I hushed him in and just fell to the floor again, crying. He held me whilst I soaked his shoulder with my tears. He smelt of beer I thought, must have been drinking over the waste ground near our houses; that was where all the kids went to underage drink.

I couldn't speak at first just sat there in silence but he pulled me close to his chest and kissed me on my head totally missing my forehead but kissing my hair I felt so comforted by that and then everything came blurting out of me. I told him what had happened with Malcolm and that he was sitting in the front room downstairs having a coffee with my mum. He went to fly out of my room but I caught his arm and begged him not to say anything or do anything it would make things worse. I just wanted to forget about it. He made me promise not to go back there, which is a promise I did keep and said that he needed to be locked up, killed or have his dick chopped off. I agreed with him.

Spence was so angry when he left mine, he had finally got the courage due to a few shandies to tell me how he felt unbeknown to me. He went straight to Malcolm's. Shaking as he wrote the word on the door. As soon as he started, he was not sure how to spell it. It was one of those words that was not spelled how it sounded. So, he did a shortened version of it instead. Standing back and admiring his handiwork he felt quite the graffiti artist. Now everyone would know what type of man lived here. He stuck his middle finger up. This was for India he would end up paying for what he had done to her one day.

I don't know why I kept going back after the first time it started happening. I should have realised something was wrong after that first cuddle. I never saw him cuddle any of the other kids. But then he would only touch me when no one else was around. I have always wanted to please men since then and never voiced my opinion. After that night, I went to my local hairdressers and had my long hair cut off to a shoulder length. I felt like cutting my hair would somehow make what happened go away, and also thought long hair could have been what attracted Malcolm to me in the first place. I no longer looked or felt like a little girl but my hair cut resembled a mushroom I hated it.

With Edward it is different I finally feel like I have a voice and he listens. Whether he agrees with what I have to say or not is irrelevant, but he still loves me regardless. We have that sort of relationship where we can act silly all the time, put on baby voices, and have offensive nicknames for each other that we only call each other in private. He is affectionate, and he tells me he loves me all of the time, especially when I am acting a fool. The sex was amazing too, The first time we had sex, I knew when I woke up next to him holding his hand that I would be having his babies one day. I finally enjoyed it and didn't just lay there, we would have sex at least once a day and it was the first time I had properly orgasmed I thought I had, had one before but I had never experienced nothing like this feeling it was euphoric, like I was transported to a place I had never been before that made everything all better. I would have had sex all day every day if I could, that feeling was so addictive.

Two weeks prior to the proposal I remember showing him a quote with a very cute picture of a bride and groom with the words 'marry someone you want to annoy for the rest of your life'. Shocked was an understatement when he popped the question, so much so I knocked the ring out of his hand and nearly stood on it. But I am engaged to someone who loves me despite my flaws (I have a lot) and past. Who knew he was out there? I have been waiting for him my whole life. I am now the wrong side of thirty but, hey, I'm getting married. Let the stress begin.

Proposal

February 2016 looking back I should have seen the signs. The day it took place Edward seemed very distracted; he even offered to pay to have my nails done. In hindsight, I wish I had now, as I did have to send a lot of pictures of my hand. But I didn't know he was going to propose, did I? We had arranged to go out for a meal in a quirky restaurant that I had been dying to go to, which was about half an hour's drive from where we lived, so Edward suggested staying in a hotel, that way, we could both relax and have a drink. He said he would sort it and I was impressed by his choice. It was a beautiful eighteenth century hotel set in glorious gardens and only a few minutes' drive from the restaurant perfect. He said he got a special offer and I wasn't going to complain as I was so excited to stay there. When we arrived later that afternoon I felt like we were in a period drama as the grounds around were stunning. It was towards the end of the month, nearly the start of spring, and crocuses and daffodils had already started to bloom. The room was classically decorated in neutral colours and there was a massive marble bathroom with a rain shower big enough for three. When I emerged in just a towel with my hair wet, dripping down my back, I noticed rose petals on the bed. I thought, how romantic. but then realized it said the words 'Marry Me'. Let's just say getting engaged made me incredibly horny we didn't end up making our dinner reservation ended up back in the shower but this time I wasn't alone.

For all you lucky engaged people out there, one of the first things everyone asks other than to see the ring or ask how he/she proposed, is when's the big day.

I was so lucky all my family adored Edward and his family liked me too, I think! So, everyone was ecstatic for us. The night of the proposal I hadn't told anybody as I wanted to tell our families in person, so I could see their faces. The next day we travelled to the seaside to tell my family first. They were so happy, insisted on making a celebratory roast and even brought champagne. We then saw Edward's parents on the way home, as they didn't live far from us, to share the good news, and they were thrilled too and couldn't believe it as Edward had always told them he would never get married. I called some friends. Spence was next on my list. He had tried calling me a few times in the early hours of the morning and I couldn't make out the gargled voicemails; he must have been pissed yet again, seemed to be a regular occurrence lately. I would often get the odd drunk text at five a.m. or a missed call from him, He would come up with some excuse when I would question him about him saying it wasn't meant for me or he must have pocket dialled. Here it goes. I was dreading it as I already knew what he would say: "You're rushing into it. Are you sure this man is for you?" and I was right, he sounded fine at first but then it was like he couldn't speak. He said he would call me back and ended the call abruptly. Why can't he just be happy for me, I thought.

When me and Edward first started dating, Spence would always compare him to my exes, and not in a good way. We have been out on some double dates with him and his wife and they have always had a great laugh together, they even support the same shitty football team they had a lot in common and were very similar in some ways. But it was like Spence was a different person, though, when we spoke alone, to when we were all out together I couldn't understand it. But then again, I remember thinking the exact same things when he introduced me to Sarah, with her long legs, curly red hair, green eyes and natural beauty. I just took it that he was trying to look out for me because he cared, although had a funny way of showing it sometimes. It didn't matter what he thought, anyway. This was about me for once. This was the happiest I had been for a long time; not even Spence could bring me down.

Setting the date sets everything in stone and makes it more real. Being engaged, you are in a bit of a bubble thinking of castles, designer wedding dresses, twenty plus bridesmaids. But as soon as that date is set, that all goes out of the window as you realise weddings are not free or paid for by someone else, unless you have a wedding godmother or very rich family members. The reality is a bit bleaker. I've been looking at wedding dresses on online selling sites, not glamourous at all. I realised that I am not royalty and not loaded so a wedding in a castle was out of the question, unless it was made of sand, and possibly about three bridesmaids, and I could only really afford to pay for dresses, accessories not included.

Don't you just hate people who know exactly where they want to get married even before they are engaged? They have it all planned out in their head—the venue, the dress, the honeymoon—just knowing that one day they will meet the right man and he will propose. Already have their folder full of cut outs with pictures of wedding dresses and colour schemes and their perfect groom. The funny thing is, this has happened to two people I know, and they have ended up getting married, had the perfect wedding dress, venue and honeymoon everything they had ever wanted. Perfect, perfect, perfect! I am jealous; they obviously seem to have their lives all mapped out and it goes to plan. Had parents that were still married and had the perfect childhood no Uncle Ms in sight. Don't know about you, but my life never seems to go that way, I have come to realise that life has a funny way of fucking up your plans.

I have always been very career driven and always tried to push myself to the limit in jobs that I have had. To travel the world, see the eight wonders, explore different cultures was also the plan, get some life experience; and as you can probably guess, I have never been travelling. I have been on holiday, of course, but this is not the same, sipping cocktails in a five-star resort in my eyes is not travelling. Some of you may disagree. The idea of travelling is great, but it is the reality; I am scared of everything—the dark, bugs, snakes, spiders—and I have OCD, which seemed to start after the night I lost my virginity as I felt so dirty and covered in germs and have done ever since. Anti-bacterial gel and wipes became my best friend. It is a lot better now due to medication and before my current job I worked in a school with children of nursery age. They would always have snotty noses and dirty hands and would clamber all over me, and I couldn't wash my hands every five minutes as I had children to watch. I realised that nothing bad had happened to me, like I had thought. I didn't get ill or catch a disease, nor did anyone around me, because I hadn't washed my hands.

I never wanted children. I think that's because I thought they came with marriage and that was something I had never thought would happen, so that's why I just got stuck into work. But now, over thirty, I want nothing more than to get married and have children. One person can come into your life and make you see it in a whole new light.

We wanted to celebrate with everyone, share our good news, and thought the best way was to have a party. In a way, this is like a prequel to the wedding as you have to find a venue, sort out food, decorations etcetera. First things first, very much like the wedding, we needed to set a date and then look at possible venues. We didn't want to spend too much money, so we were looking at village halls that were local or pub function rooms. We ended up booking a ballroom. It had a stage, a kitchen and a large bar with cheap drink, and also had an outside area that was okay. It was cheap to book, too. We could use all of the tables and chairs; they were a bit tatty but thought with a tablecloth and in the dark, who would know. We decided on a theme too: black, red and gold. Mainly because the chairs were red so thought that would be much easier. We got invites, which we posted to family and friends who were not local, and handed out the rest. This was not an easy decision who, to invite, as really if you invited these people to the engagement surely, they should be invited to the wedding.

We had six weeks until the party I had ordered decorations online. My sister, Chynna, had said she would be in charge of photographs and even made a banner saying "soon to be the James". I showed this to Edward who went completely white, like he had seen a ghost. I think he was having a freak out about the whole, getting married thing; it was like this shit just got real.

The day of the party came around so quickly. My family came up during the day to help us decorate. I thought with us all being there it would take about an hour, but I was very much mistaken. It took a lot longer than that. We didn't have enough tablecloths. I didn't know where to put the tables or where to hang photographs and banners. This party had caused me so much stress. Edward did say to me that he would organise the rest of the wedding as he could only imagine what I would be like if this was anything to go by. I had spent a week before making a post box for cards. If I had known it was going to take that long, I would have brought one, saved myself the hassle, and I got three-D letters of our initials, which I had decorated and put them on a table by themselves surrounded by confetti and candles, but it looked more like a tribute at a funeral. I didn't have time now, just had to do what we could. The black and gold theme was a bad idea I wished I had just gone for white and another colour. Coloured cutlery, plates, containers, serviettes were so much more expensive than white ones and were hard to find. We put a centre piece of red, gold and black balloons and a bowl of sweets on every table, with a decorative gold vase with fairy lights in. It looked a bit shit, not how I had imagined, but I didn't have time to mess about. No one would care anyway. Soon it would be dark and everyone would be pissed.

I had been trying to get hold of Spence all day, but he wasn't returning my calls or messages. He was meant to be coming up during the day to help decorate as him and Sarah were staying in a nearby hotel so they could both drink. Who knows what happened to him? That was the other problem with parties. We invited a hundred people who, all apart from a handful, said they were coming. But what if they didn't turn up? Every time my phone rang on the day, I thought that was someone cancelling and was anxious that this very big ballroom would look very empty. We had also catered for a hundred people and with the help of family again did everything ourselves. We had so much food it was unreal, everything from chicken nuggets to popcorn. Lucky, we had a kitchen onsite as most of the food was still in there as we already had so much out. We had asked a friend to make a cake for us who was given free rein, just given the colour scheme.

We had wasted practically a whole day getting the venue ready which didn't leave a lot of time for us to actually get ready. It's so much easier for men all they need to do is shower and change. Edward didn't have to do his hair either, as he had none, so he got ready in a flash. I don't know about you, but this always happens to me. I never seem to have time to get ready, even if I hadn't been at the venue all day and I had spent the whole day doing nothing I would have still managed to leave myself no time. I had the quickest shower possible, just quickly washed the important bits, slung on a tight-fitting red dress which was my sister's—it was slightly too small but due to the design held me in and gave me the best cleavage ever—and paired it with some black strappy sandals. I curled my shoulder length hair so it looked like spirals, which made it spring up to above my ears. It will drop, I thought, well, I hoped it would as I didn't have time to rewash and do it all again. I stuck on fake eyelashes and was ready to go; I would have to do.

We arrived early so we could get the food that was in the fridge out and have a quick drink before everyone arrived. The DJ started to set up and when the music started friends and family started to arrive. I was nervous about this night as Edward would be meeting some of my friends and family for the first time and vice versa. Would they like me, would they like Edward? More people and then more people arrived. I kept my coat on as I was very self-conscious about my tits, they looked so huge, I wasn't used to getting them out.

More people and then more people arrived. I didn't have to buy a drink everyone kept buying me one, but I would put it down as someone else arrived that I had to greet. To be honest it was hard work, trying to make sure everyone was okay, trying to make conversation. Meeting friend's partners for the first time. I had lost my bag so hopefully no one was trying to ask for directions as my phone was in there. Sorting out the food, there was not enough seating, as I think eighty people turned up in the end and most of them sat down in groups, a table of work colleagues, family, school friends, for example. I was so surprised, but even though we had a lot of guests we way over did the food as it had been hardly touched. I think because the booze was cheap, they would rather drink than eat. Until later on when all you want to do is eat after you have a skinful and a kebab is like the best food in the world, until you wake up with kebab stuck to the side of your face in the morning as you have fallen asleep eating it.

All my bridesmaids were there helping me, and Edward entertained, dancing with the children and requesting songs from Britney and Whitney to dance to. Spence turned up two hours late, without Sarah and pissed as a fart. What was he playing at and where had he been all day? I should have been happy that he was there and not dead after going missing for the day, but he was making a show of himself. He knew how important tonight was. This would be the first time both our families met properly. My family were all on their best behaviour, I didn't recognise them at all and my mum reckoned she had twelve whiskeys as she was nervous too. I barely saw Edward that night, only when we had to pose for photographs and cut the cake but it felt like an actual wedding. Should have just got married then; it would have been easier and more relaxed. We were both being social butterflies and I had been outside for most of the evening with a very drunken Spence. He owed me big time for this and I wouldn't let him forget it in a hurry. I even had a fag as I was stressed out, I did occasionally have a slip up especially if I was drunk as I had given up. It tasted bloody disgusting and I instantly regretted it.

Edward's best man made him do a speech in front of everyone, so he thanked everyone for coming and then gushed about me of course. It was so lovely. He said that I made him a better person and I knew exactly what he meant, as he made me feel that way too, but I was embarrassed and hid behind him like a child, so no one could see me. He was six foot two and I was five feet, after all; most of the time you can't see me. Spence walked out during the speech, which was rude, I thought. When I asked him, he said he needed air and then he started saying in his drunken state, he told me he'd had an argument with Sarah, that's why she didn't come. It's funny how drink can bring out feelings and honesty. I ended up putting him in a cab and sending him back to her to try and sort things out. As I opened the car door to shove him in, he whispered in my ear, "I love you," and I jokingly replied tapping his nose, "And I love you too," even though you are a drunken mess, I thought.

Later that night after the last guest had gone, we had cleared the majority of the venue and chucked the food in the bins. Such a waste. The few remaining family and friends were heading into town to make a night of it as it was only just after twelve. I was absolutely shattered, there was no way I could go out and party now. God, I had got so old, lol. Me and Edward got a taxi and on the short ride home all I could think about was what Spence had said.

The Venue

After the party we had pondered on the idea of going abroad doing the whole get married in Vegas and then come back and have a reception. Walking down the aisle to an Elvis impersonator singing *Fools Rush In*, in a little makeshift chapel on the Sunset Strip. But weighing up the pros and cons we decided to do it here. We may regret it later down the line, but the main reason was so we could have everyone we wanted there for the main bit, getting married, not just for the piss up afterwards.

So, the date was set. 21st of September. The first thing really that you need to sort out is a venue. Unless you already know where you want to get married then you may have to change your date to suit them. We had viewed some possible venues and gone to some wedding open days but none of them felt right. There was always something wrong, whether it be where the toilets were situated or that you got married in one place and then had to take a long walk to the reception. I did like the idea of getting married in a church and there was a church I had driven past a few times quite near to our home which would look beautiful in photographs. My hubby to be wasn't too keen as he wasn't religious, but then nor was I, but I said it couldn't hurt having a look. I found the vicar's details online and called him to see what we needed to do to get married there. Our first hurdle was that we weren't in their parish. Our parents and grandparents hadn't got married there either so to marry there we would need to attend for a few months prior to the wedding. Okay, so this was not ideal as we led busy lives and done shift work, but least we had a chance. The vicar was down to earth, funny and sounded young on the phone not how I imagined at all. He said to come to a service and see what it was like first, as he said that his way was not for everyone. I couldn't wait. I was super excited. Edward did not share my feelings.

The following Sunday me, my mum, dad, Chynna and Edward arrived at the church. The entrance was arched with wooden doors, stained glass windows and a huge cross on the roof, all lit up, and it smelt of wood. As soon as I walked in, I thought of Malcolm; not the best start. It was the smell first that reminded me of him, and then the bare wooden frame of the balcony took me back to a time I felt like I was being watched. I had this feeling every time I used the toilet in Malcolm's empty echoey house. It was supposedly haunted, so maybe I was.

There had been stories over the years about that house, and the road the houses had been built on, that it was cursed, that it use to be an old burial ground. I sometimes would get an overpowering smell of lavender like how my nan once smelled, but no grannies were in sight; or I would get an overwhelming scent of smoke, which also reminded me of my nan as she always had a fag in her mouth, even was buried with a packet of fags. I don't think no one thought to put a lighter in her coffin though, so fuck knows how she was going to light it.

Things happened at home too. I would sometimes hear the sound of someone walking up the stairs when my mum and my siblings were all fast asleep in bed. When my nan become unwell I knew something was wrong as her picture fell from the wall. This had happened before when my grandad had died. A psychic once came to the area and said it was naughty spirit children lighting fires. That explained the burning smell, but not the flowers. None of the children or Spence had the same feelings or smell and thought I was doing it for attention. They knew I was Malcolm's favourite as he would always single me out and make me work alone or near where he would be, and would pay me more money. Little did the other kids know that he was probably paying me extra because he was doing extra things to me. I even felt eyes on me when I was using the loo. I would always be told to use the toilet upstairs, even though there was one downstairs that all the other kids used. Okay, the one upstairs was bigger, but it had bare creaky flooring and only part of the door frame was finished so above the door the glass panel was missing. It smelled of wood, like old wood, like the church did, and I knew now I would never be able to get married here as the last person I wanted to be reminded of on the wedding day was Malcolm. I did try to avoid using the loo there as much as possible as the door didn't have a lock on the inside either, so anyone could have walked in. I would quickly run in and go trying to hold the door shut with my leg, just in case someone accidently tried getting in. This would be a regular occurrence on nights out on the town when I was over eighteen because pubs and nightclub toilets that I seemed to use never had locks on. You would either have to hold your leg up against the door whilst trying to pee and not get it everywhere, or always go to the loo with your friend so they could either come in with you or hold their foot under the door.

The church was on a busy main road and was opposite some fast-food places but would still look nice in photographs. I wanted the family to come for their opinion too as they were a big part of the day. But as soon as I walked in and thought of Malcolm, it definitely was not the place to get married. I think I had lost most of them anyway as soon as we walked through the door, as it was freezing, but it had a warmth to it as everyone was very welcoming and friendly. We were even offered tea, coffee and biscuits which was nice. My mum was loving it. They had a band playing right next to the alter and a girl singing who thought she was auditioning for a singing competition. It was a lovely church but I couldn't shake Malcolm. It was like he was there watching me or maybe this time it was my nan or spirits; there were graves outside. I wish it had been spirits watching me at Malcolm's and not him on a ladder watching me pee. I sang hymns and tried joining in even with the prayers but it was useless, this place was definitely a no-no.

I couldn't gauge what the rest thought other than my mum, but to my relief, other than my mum, everyone hated it. Edward said that he had more fun counting the stiches on the back of a coat on the man stood on front of him. Oh well, at least we tried, but could safely say from this point a church was not an option.

Before I started the venue journey, I thought I was going to be so laid back about it. I know I didn't have a clue what I exactly wanted, just somewhere pretty with appealing grounds, but when I started looking, I realised I wanted so much more.

1. Smoking area—I didn't smoke any more unless very, very drunk but a lot of my friends and family did so a smoking area near the main reception room would be preferable. This was so guests wouldn't be too far away from everything that was going on. It needed to be pleasant and sheltered with seating, but not too comfortable, so everyone spent most of their time outside, as you do need people to fill the area or you will look like you have no friends.

2. Toilets—As a woman with standards and slight OCD, the toilets had to be clean, spacious, as I may be

wearing a big dress. Also, you need room to touch your make up, have a chat with friends etcetera. I once went on a coach trip to France which took forever. the toilets on the coach stank so I didn't want to use them, so thought I would use the toilet when we got there. What I didn't realise was it was only a booze/fag coach trip. Should have guessed as all the other passengers' skin on their faces looked like it was made of leather and they all looked so old and had loads of deep lines around the mouth from too much sucking. So, when we got there, there was only a supermarket and the toilet was worse than ones I had seen in Hong Kong, when they were just holes in the ground. The walls looked like they were smeared with shit and there was no toilet seat. I was busting but ended up holding it until we got all the way home from France. So, as you can see the toilets had to be of an acceptable standard.

3. Accommodation—We had a lot of family coming to the wedding and they were not local, and our little two-bed terraced house had no room really for anyone to stay and no parking, as sometimes we even struggled having two cars. So, we either needed somewhere that had rooms onsite or places nearby that were reasonably priced and easy to get too.

All these things were important, but these were just general add-ons. This was without considering the actual ceremony room, reception and food.

Cutting weeks of hunting short and viewing many wedding venues later, we were virtually on the verge of giving up and eloping—if only we had done this at the start—but then as if by complete and utter chance, we found one that had all my boxes ticked. It had everything I wanted and more. We could have everything in one place, easier for us and guests so they wouldn't need to travel. It would save money as wouldn't need a posh wedding car. They do food and drinks packages as well and remember my priorities? Well, they were all covered. The toilets, well, they were roomy, bigger than the downstairs of my house. Big enough to fit a bride in a big dress and her bathroom helper as I was thinking I might need someone to hold my dress whilst using the toilet. This would be one of my bridesmaids' list of duties. It even had a sofa to sit on, very posh, also good for naps and/or drunken conversations.

Everything was in one place too, so the smokers were literally outside the main reception area and would still be able to hear what was going on and wouldn't make the place look empty if they all decided to go for a fag at the same time. The bar was also in the room too, so our guests wouldn't have to go elsewhere to get a drink, and it was a hotel with plenty of rooms available, more rooms than guests, and I could stay the night before too, which was ideal. Me and my bridesmaids could get ready and the suite was like an apartment, with a bedroom, bathroom, two toilets, a living area and a dining room, even an outside area with a stream running through it; and it was traditionally decorated, what you would expect of a luxury hotel. I would keep drunken guests away from the stream, and definitely my mother after she has had a few.

As I mentioned it was a hotel. On the outside it looked like a small manor house or lodge, very pretty, but inside it was quite art deco style, very 1920s, and had some unusual furnishings. The hotel reception had a beautiful parquet staircase and a big open fireplace, and they also had a spa on site. The carpet was colourful and floral, very 1980s pub, and would hide a multitude of sins. Which was good, because you don't want somewhere too posh that you are scared to have a good time just in case you spill a drink or drop some food. You literally wouldn't see a stain if you dropped anything, the carpet was so patterned. It had character and an aged sort of smell to it that I had smelled somewhere before, just couldn't figure out where.

It was funny because it was the last place we viewed as a wild card really, and the one that we loved the most. It's like when I first met my future hubby for the first time. I knew that he was the one from the moment I first spent time with him and there was that instant attraction. I will never forget it. That's how I feel about this venue. Hopefully it wouldn't rain. It was very picturesque outside so good for photographs. They had a contingency plan in place, too, if it did rain. They even showed us some photos that had been taken on such occasion when it had pissed it down.

The staff were friendly and had a lot of experience with weddings there, so I knew I was in safe hands and could relax a bit at least. They said that they would help us too in any way they could and recommended a lot of other wedding suppliers for things like flowers and cake, so had been a godsend.

I will say too that my hubby to be wasn't leaving everything down to me to sort out either, which I didn't know if it was a good or a bad thing. Obviously he didn't like the church, but nor did I, due to the memories it brought back, but he seemed to have an opinion on every other wedding venue we went to. But to be honest it all helped with the whole process. He was very practical when it came to things like that and it showed he cared. Like for example, one place was stunning but difficult to find, and quite remote. We had to take into account weather and also not everyone has a sat nav, especially the older generation. Hopefully it won't snow in September, but you get my drift. The venue is easy to get to, no back roads or windy streets, so people would still be able to get there in such event. I know it might seem that a lot of the thinking involved with this venue was choosing what would be good for everyone else, but I did think it needed to be considered as we wanted our friends and family to be able to stay at the venue and not pay the earth, not pay too much for drinks, be able to park easily, not have to travel from one venue to the next because that's a pain if you want to drink. Not have to travel too far too either.

All the input I got though was good because these were things that would never have entered my head. I liked the fact that I had an involved groom. To be honest, he was very organised, so much so that if there was a programme *Don't Tell the Groom*, I would be on it as I am useless with stuff like this as I am so indecisive, and since we have started looking, even more so.

This venue suited both of us. Edward's list of priorities were in a slightly different order from mine as he was interested in the size of the bar, what alcohol they stocked, what beer they had on tap and how many bar staff would be working. Need I say more. We were not doing a free bar as we didn't want to be made bankrupt, but also price of drinks was something to consider too, as it was an expensive day not just for us, but for guests too.

The Guest Lists

Venue sorted, now comes the guest list; this is going to be fun. Who is worth a hundred pounds for the day, that is the question? Also, we have to pay for ourselves, which is a bit of a liberty I thought. Save the dates need to be written and sent out as soon as possible so guests can book the time off etcetera. Once these are sent too you know this is final as they will expect an invite to the day. I'm not going to send these to the evening guests. There has been lots of thoughts going through my head like will I still be speaking to this person next year; would they invite me to their wedding. Did they bother turning up to the engagement? Have I actually seem them this year? This wouldn't be an issue if we got married in a registry office and had hired a hall but at this venue we were paying per head. I was happy when I found out there was some family drama too because less people to invite lol. How bad am I?

Surely a wedding should just be about me and the groom, right? Wrong, it's about everyone else. Trying to please them, paying out for them. In hindsight we should have just gone abroad. I suppose we still could as only paid a deposit. Don't tempt me! The other thing we had to sort out was food. We were given a large menu by the venue with loads of different packages on. There were ones for drinks, canapes, children and for the wedding breakfast. I have always wondered why it's called a wedding breakfast as you don't get a full English and it's not usually in the morning when you would normally have breakfast, but the name is claimed to have come from pre-reformation times, when the wedding service was usually held after mass and the bride and groom would have had to fast before that, so after the ceremony the priest would hand out food and drink that he had blessed.

So, would we go for food that we liked or try to order something that everyone would find appealing? I had been to a few weddings and had a three course sit down meal that I had slated. I hadn't realized how much the newlyweds had to pay for it. So I knew my guests would probably feel the same. We also had to cater for vegans, vegetarians and gluten free.

Anyone who has already planned a wedding, I salute you as it is a lot harder that it looks. I was very lucky to have a super organised groom, and since booking the venue he had practically sorted out all the main things, even done a spreadsheet of deposits we had paid, what was outstanding and when we needed to pay it. I was useless when it came to these sorts of things, let's put it this way: I didn't pay the bills, change energy suppliers, sort out insurance etcetera. I'm sure my partner loves having that responsibility. I was involved, mind you. I was in control of the more girlie things like hair, makeup, bridesmaid dresses, flowers, centre pieces. You get my drift. I don't know about you, but as soon as you mention the word wedding the price triples. It's ludicrous that on a normal day you could order a bouquet for thirty pounds but this same bouquet on your wedding day was a hundred pounds plus. Did they use super flowers that never died? No, they didn't, it was because you mentioned the W word. It wasn't not just florists; it was venues, food and entertainment. I did wonder how anyone afforded to get married these days, but I knew of course people did, but at what cost?

I sometimes wished I had been born in a different era where there wasn't all this pressure and you had limited choices—get married in a church or registry office—and you had the reception at your mum and dad's house or a hall. Well, that's how it was in my family anyway. My mum got married at twenty-three, wore a second-hand wedding dress, got married in a beautiful little church and then had a reception at my nan and grandad's house. They even had a make shift bar in the garden. What more could you want?

Looking back at photographs it looked perfect, but I felt like it was more a competition now to see who could have the most extravagant wedding and spend the most money, because it was obvious that was what made a good wedding. Of course, you wanted your wedding to stand out and be original, but it didn't have to cost a fortune. I thought about Spence and how he had used all of his savings to pay for the dream wedding that Sarah wanted and look at them now; they were having problems. At the end of the day, it was one day. Think how quickly one day goes; whether you spent thousands of pounds or you didn't, the outcome would still be the same: you would be married to the person you loved—or in my case want to annoy—for the rest of your life. Did you really want to start married life in debt, unless you have savings? But wouldn't you rather put a deposit on a house if you didn't own one already, or buy a new car, or even have an amazing honeymoon? That was what it came down to, I suppose, personal preference. On the other hand, you could look at it that you were only going to do this once so go all out, fireworks the lot. Anyway, these were just a few thoughts going through my head now. My indecisiveness had increased, and I changed my mind from one day to the next. I had bride brain, if that was a thing. I hoped this would be my debt free journey to I do.

Having a wedding had made me realise I didn't have a lot of real friends. I had work colleagues, but I wouldn't class them as friends as such, maybe one or two, but there were not people I really spoke to outside of work. Sure, I said the whole "hi, how are you" when I saw them, but would I invite them to my wedding?

Also, something else bothering me was this whole plus one thing. Everyone that you invited who was single, did they get one? I hadn't a clue. My sister asked me, and I just said it depended on numbers really, as it was costing a lot as it was and I suppose it depended on who it is. A lot could happen in a year, couldn't it? You could fall pregnant and have a baby in that time. Oh god, what if I fell pregnant and was too fat to fit in my dress?

Had to have a crisis meeting in the end with our wedding planner, needed to ask about cutting costs, gluten free, lighting and wanted another look round, really. But of course there had to be a problem, they were only refurbishing the whole hotel beforehand. What if it wasn't finished in time or looked hideous? Why didn't they tell us this when we paid the deposit? They assured us that it would all be fine so I had to trust them I guess. Didn't really have another choice now did we?

That stress aside the whole who to invite part was stressing me out. I had written a rough list of about two hundred people, but they were just people I wanted to invite. The problem was the plus ones also as you were paying for someone to have a plus one when you may not have even met them. You wouldn't pay for your friend and their date to eat and drink all day at a restaurant, so why would you at a wedding?

I thought I could probably write a book on this subject. So immediate family not a problem, loved them and spent a lot of time with them. There were some family members, aunties, uncles and cousins, that I saw a few times a year. Aunties that had been coming and going all my life. Cousins who I spent a lot of time with when little but now hadn't spoken to in years. Who did you invite? Mum and Dad were divorced but luckily still were on pretty good terms. They could be in the same room as each other, just about. Sometimes I thought fuck the rest of both the families, which I knew might sound harsh, but I thought, who did I see? Who tried to make an effort? To make matters worse, on both sides of the family my mum's and dad's, there was aggravation which had pros and cons, as there were less people to invite. But my mum was a fence sitter so spoke to all her sisters and brothers, but one brother didn't speak to two sisters. One sister didn't speak to the other and so on and so on. It was the same on my dad's side now, which I thought I would never say as they had always got along. But now things were getting juicy. One sister had an argument with a brother then another sister stepped in, then the kids started and now it was all chaos like my mum's family, one not talking to the other. Which made it so difficult when it came to who to invite. I needed help. Did I just invite everyone as then I wouldn't look like the bad guy and then hope that most of them didn't turn up?

The Dress

Most women would say that this was the most important part of the day and it needed to be right or the day would be ruined. But I had watched enough reality TV to know that wasn't the case. Their dress could be shit but they still managed to have a good day regardless.

For me my main priority was being able to go for a wee in my dress, sounds stupid I know, but I didn't want to be having to worry every time I went to the loo that I needed a chaperone to help me, not at all glamorous. I had even had a look online to see ways to wee in your wedding dress. Have a look if you don't believe me; they are good reads. All joking aside, I had never dreamed of the perfect dress since setting the date. I had to be more practical. I did have a look at a few online as you do, and nosed about a few shop windows, and realised I was not that fussy. I thought most of the dresses I had seen were pretty in one way or another, and I thought only by trying them on would I know what I liked and what suited me. It wasn't the dress that worried me, it was what the person who would be wearing the dress would look like. Me!

I had always been a worrier ever since I can remember but since setting the date, my worrying had gone into overdrive.

I was the sort of person who worried if I was not worrying about anything. I then had to find something to worry about. I wished I was the sort of person who didn't give a fuck, and I had tried to change the way I thought by doing cognitive behavioural therapy, which didn't help, I think mainly because I wasn't honest enough with myself. But in the end I thought it was just the way I was, and I had got to accept it.

Today was no exception. I was going to try on wedding dresses for the first time. For most women this would be a happy day, but I was anxious, I think more because my mum and sister were coming, and my mum had no filter, so much so she once told a wedding dress shop owner at a wedding open day we went to that one of her two-thousand-pound dresses looked like a cheap pair of net curtains. I could have literally died on the spot and what made it worse was the fact that I really quite liked it.

So, we set off and I was driving. I hated driving; sometimes I wished I had never passed my test. I had found the shop online and I liked the look of a couple of dresses and they were reasonably priced too. Your reasonable and my reasonable may be somewhat different, so I was thinking a thousand pounds and below, but being honest, I was hoping I wouldn't spend nearly that much. I seemed to have every programme that had wedding or bride in the title series linked just for ideas, I had seen a lot of women on TV trying on wedding dresses and getting very emotional, knowing that this dress was the one, so I had high expectations. I wanted tears, not only from my eyes, but from my mum's and sister's.

We arrived half an hour late for the appointment as I could not find this bloody shop. I had driven around in circles and could not see it. In the end I got my mum to phone them for directions. Modern day technology was on too, sat nav on my phone, and still, I couldn't find it. When we finally found it, it was in the middle of this quaint little village and it wasn't a shop at all, it was a house. Yes, you heard correct, a house. I did think for a second that the website must have been fake; I had images in my head that made day turn into night. Suddenly rain came out of nowhere, so we ran for the door, it opened and as we peered round and said hello, we were grabbed by an evil killer who would make us meet our bitter end. I could see the news headlines, "Brides to be nowhere to be seen", as this killer had a thing for the newly engaged.

I had quite an imagination, as you can probably tell. Anyway, going back to it, I pulled onto the drive and could have cried, I was so stressed. I was stressed enough before but now I was on another level. I know I wanted tears but not due to stress and anxiety.

A lady answered the door. I hated being late—it was one of my pet hates—so firstly I apologised. I was all sweaty too. It was April and quite a warm day, but I was not sweating from the heat. It was stress sweat. I remember thinking the shop must be round the back or something but sadly I was wrong. It was a room out the back of the garage with three very long rails of wedding dresses and a very small two-seater sofa in the corner. There did not seem to be a changing room; this was awkward. Okay, so my mum and sister had obviously seen me naked at some point but let's just say I wasn't looking my best and not the most body confident. But maybe there was a separate room for changing, that's what I hoped. But no, there wasn't, of course there wasn't, so the lady asked me to pick a few dresses off the racks and then she would come back in ten minutes and I could try them.

I hoped she wasn't going to help me get changed as I didn't want a stranger to see me naked. I did not like anyone seeing me naked, even Edward, due to the hang ups I had about my body and the thought of someone staring at me took me back to Malcolm's house when he would watch me. The rails were quite high, so the dresses were not dragging on the floor, and I had not been blessed with height being five foot; nor had my mum who was even smaller. My sister had a couple of inches on us, but we still struggled to even get the dresses off.

I did not have a clue where to start. Three walls of dresses all crammed in together and not in any kind of order or size. I picked out three, all different: one lace, one strapless and one with a lot of bling and beaded, all beautiful in their own kind of way. The lady came back in and basically asked me to strip off there and then. I took my clothes off, leaving myself in my strapless bra and knickers, so I stood there in the cold practically naked in front of the woman, my mum and sister, while I had to step into the first dress. There was a mirror, thank god, so I could see what I looked like, but there was no grand entrance moment like I had always imagined, coming out from the changing room and everyone going wow. I was there, about two feet away from everyone. There was no amazing moment and the dress was awful. I didn't know if it was my face that made it look awful, but it was like some granny dress. Apologies grannies, no offence intended. I would usually love a granny dress, but not on my wedding day. Maybe it was because the dress was lace and not fitted, but honestly, I have never felt uglier and I could see my mum's and sister's faces not smiling, like trying to be polite, saying they liked the back.

I couldn't even bear to look at myself in the mirror I felt that disgusting. I felt like I was in fancy dress or trying on my mum's clothes when I was little.

The back looked nice, just what I wanted to hear. I have an extremely dodgy tattoo on my back, so awful that you can't even tell what it is. Most people ask me what country I have tattooed on my back but it's actually a dragon, but I had found myself saying Ireland more often than not, as it was easier. I was sixteen when

I had it done, underage and rebellious. I had grown up quickly due to my past and started going clubbing from as soon as I could get in. The local nightclub in the town never asked me for ID, well, not until I passed out in the toilet after having too much to drink and being pulled out by the bouncer. He asked me my age and of course I stupidly replied sixteen. I couldn't get in after that so thought with my young mind that you had to be eighteen to get a tattoo so if I had one they should let me in again. I had seen a tattoo I really liked. It was like a sun outline with a hole in the middle, but black. I had been looking around and done some research. By research, I mean going into tattoo parlours and flicking through there catalogues of images, and I found one that I fell in love with, which was very similar, but had a black dragon in the middle and was filled in red. I didn't want to do anything too hasty as tattoos are for life, well, at the time they were. You never heard of anyone having laser treatment then or a cover up job.

A few weeks had passed, and I decided yes, this was the tattoo for me. So, me and my friend went to the shop where I found the picture and of course it was closed. I had worked myself up for it so today was the day I was getting one, so went to another tattoo shop and told them what it was I wanted. Remember, I was underage, but I didn't get asked for ID, the tattoo artist just said that there were some dragon pictures in one of the books. They were nothing like I hoped but I just picked a dragon, all black, and said I would have that.

He said that would be fine, but advised me to have a couple of stiff drinks first and then come back, due to it being all black ink work. Bearing in mind I was sixteen and it was ten o'clock in the morning, not the best advice, but off I went. I went to a pub where they opened early and served beer with breakfast. It was part of a chain, so I knew that I would be able to get a drink there. I had a couple of Scotches—that was my favourite underage drink of choice then, mainly because Mum and Dad drank it so both would have it at home and could be easily topped up with water if I stole some— and went back.

I sat in a chair, straddled, as I was having it on my back, and he started. The rest is a blur. I felt sick so had to hold a bin in front of me and for about ten minutes my vision was blurred, and I went deaf. I didn't know if it was the Scotch or the tattoo or a combination of both, but I got through it, just. It wasn't painful at all, just a burning sensation. If I didn't feel sick, lose my hearing or vision, I think it would have been fine. I instantly regretted it and have done ever since. I should have listened to my mum, she had known best this time, although I would never admit to it and I never did get back in the nightclub until I was of legal age so getting the tattoo didn't make me look older.

Going back to the dress, I did not want a dress that had a nice back as I didn't want to highlight my dodgy tattoo.

My sister took a couple of pics of me in the dresses, but looking at them later, wished she hadn't as I looked worse in the picture than I did in the mirror. I wasn't the most photogenic.

Moving swiftly on, I tried on the next one, so stripped again. This one was a bit better, fitted nicely had a fishtail, strapless sweetheart neckline, but I still didn't have that feeling and there were no tears in the room. I think the lady thought this was the one, though, as the next thing I knew, she was putting a veil on my head, making me put on some used ill-fitting shoes to give me a bit of height. I smiled politely and said I liked the shape but there was just something missing. A tiara maybe, she said. No, not what I was thinking at all. I was unsure if I wanted to wear a veil, but a tiara was a definite no, no.

Then onto the final one. It was my favourite and hugged my curvy figure and actually looked quite nice, if I did say so myself. My mum and sister liked it too, but there was no real emotion, so I knew it wasn't the one, one. But the best of a bad bunch. This experience wasn't one I would be repeating anytime soon, but one thing that I had gained from it was what styles suited me and that I was open to anything really, I even liked a lot of the dresses with bling which surprised me as before going, I wasn't too keen. I also noted to myself for next time to make sure my hair looked nice and my make-up was done, as it was hard to like anything when you looked like shit. Also, to make sure I took heels, the sort of height I thought I would be wearing as it did make a difference. But try on all different styles, not just one you think you will like, as you will be surprised and probably find the shape that you were not that keen on will be the one. If I was to give any advice to anyone dress hunting, go with an open mind, you will be surprised that what you think you want doesn't suit you so try on dresses outside of your comfort zone. You never know, you might like them. Plus, one other thing, when you are booking wedding dress appointments, make sure they are legit dress shops. Don't want anyone to have to go through what I did.

I had been looking on selling sites as you do, just to look for cheap wedding bundles, centrepieces, trying to grab a bargain, when I saw a wedding dress near enough identical to the last one, I'd tried on in the shop, sorry, I meant house. It was seventy pounds, brand new and my size. It did sound too good to be true, but I messaged the woman. I had, had a look at the dress online and saw that the same dress was being sold for around five hundred pounds, so I thought even if it didn't look nice, I could always sell it on and make some money.

All these business ideas started running through my mind. I thought about turning my spare room into a wedding dress shop. If that women could do it, so could I. I would offer tea and coffee, too and put the heating on, and clearly state that it wasn't a shop, it was a house. Anyway, all hopes were dashed when the lady emailed back to say that the dress had been sold. Gutted, I was, but now I had it in my head that this couldn't be the only dress that was being sold cheaply so carried on looking online and found the same identical dress in my size, a bit pricier at a hundred and eighty pounds. I messaged the lady and she still had it, but said it needed to go that night. I said I would go and look at it, so off I went. It was beautiful, just like the picture, so I bought it there and then. So, then I had a dress that I hadn't even tried on but looked nice on the tall slim model in the picture online. I was the opposite, so it would definitely need altering as I was a short arse. I liked the back of the dress as it was corset style so would be ideal if I put on any weight as I could let it out, as my big fear was back fat.

I couldn't wait to show my sister and mum and they thought it was stunning. I just prayed it looked as good on me on the day, once altered.

I had been also making an epic fail when it came to my dress. I was too honest for my own good. Everyone who asked me about it, I blurted out I got it from a selling site for a hundred and eighty pounds and did they want to see a picture. Not even just close family and friends, just everyone. Was this bad luck? I hoped not, because I was not the luckiest person in the world already I knew it was bad luck for the groom to see it, but unsure about everyone else. I didn't even register that it would even be until someone was shocked when I just showed them.

Bridesmaids

It's weird how when you get engaged some friends just assume that they will be a bridesmaid and you always must have that awkward conversation with the ones who aren't. This is nothing like the film, sorry to disappoint.

Picking bridesmaids is a lot harder than I thought it would be. Some are no brainers and just expect to be asked. When you are working to a budget it's even harder. If money was no object, I would just ask all my friends. I didn't want to be a tight bride where I ask them to buy their own dresses as I think that is something a bride needs to provide. I think, though, the title bridesmaid needs to change to bride slave, as really, your bridesmaids are there to work for no money at all. They must obviously plan your hen do, wear a dress that is inferior to yours, compliment you constantly, not look as nice as you on the day, and any other jobs in between. On the day they will be practically working unpaid, so providing a dress is the least I can do.

For any of you that have been a bridesmaid already, you will know that it is hard work and longer than a day's work, as you are constantly the go to girl on the day and the days leading up to it. You have to be on hand for dress fittings, hen do, help with wedding hair, wedding make up and flowers... the list goes on. I was happy to be asked to be a bridesmaid as. As an adult this was my first time, but a thirty-year-old bridesmaid is not really attractive. I was so much cuter as my younger self, although I had lost my front two teeth, which didn't look great in photos and that was when I loved having all the attention so was in a lot of photos. My job back then was only to look cute. It changes as you get older.

I called one of my oldest friends, Jodie, and told her I was engaged the morning after it happened and after her first two questions—'what is the ring like' and 'how did he propose'—she said, "Send me a picture," which proves my earlier points. It wasn't even a question really. It was like, "I'm going to be bridesmaid," there was no question that she wouldn't be, but I wanted to ask her in the correct way, send her a card or a present saying, 'will you be my bridesmaid?', but she beat me too it. I think she was more excited than me. I was to be her bridesmaid in a few months. I was lucky as she had good taste and didn't want her bridesmaids to look ugly. We had our say on the dresses and she would always send across ideas. Some were a joke but I actually liked them. I also got to pick my colour.

I met her at junior school, now thirty-three, she had been a constant in my life. She was pretty, funny, short like me, and had hair for days. Everyone thought she wore extensions but it was natural, other than the ombre dye job. She lived a street away from me growing up, too. We tried our first fag together, bunked off school and dyed each other's hair.

I wanted to be a nice bride, not a bridezilla and give my bridesmaids choice, and not choose dresses that I liked, but ones that they liked too, as they would have to wear them. I always knew what colour I wanted but for style I was open to ideas.

Anyway, more to the point, one down, or technically two, because my sister obviously would be my chief bridesmaid/maid of honour. A lot of people think that you can't be maid of honour if you are married but you can. Maid of honour unmarried, matron of honour if you are. Who knew, so two down. The only problem was you needed bridesmaids that would not upstage the bride, but my sister would upstage me in a binbag.

We were very different looking. Chynna was taller than me, in proportion, slim, beautiful, full lips, cute nose and gorgeous chocolatey skin, with long straight hair, the total opposite of me. I am one of four siblings all younger. My sister was the closest to me in age and then I had two younger brothers, Taran and Isaiah. We were all very close. Edward had already asked my brothers to be groomsman, as he got on really well with both of them, which was really nice to see. He was also close to Chynna. I had a step sister, too. Edward didn't get on with her as much. To be fair, she was a bit of a bitch. To put it bluntly, another Debbie downer, like Spence, when it came to me and Edward, and funnily enough her name was Debbie. My step-mum was a bit better now we were older as she didn't have to have us round every weekend, but she hated us when we were kids, my dad couldn't spend a quid on us without her getting the hump. Debbie came as part of the package unfortunately. I never really liked her but mainly because my dad had a good relationship with her. She didn't see her real dad so spent a lot more time with him than I had, but I felt I had to ask her to be a bridesmaid for my dad's sake.

Edward had young nieces so thought it would be nice to ask them to be bridesmaids, as they were adorable, and I thought it was cute to have little ones in lovely dresses. I hadn't got any nieces or nephews yet and all my cousins who were little and young were now eighteen. I didn't get to ask them properly as someone beat me to it, but the next time I saw them they were super excited and couldn't wait to go shopping. We had a look online to see what sort of dresses they liked the look of and surprisingly they liked very fitted numbers. I thought they would want big poufy dresses so they looked like mini princesses. They were both under ten but growing all the time, so I decided to leave the shopping for dresses to nearer the time, to save on alterations.

I did have other friends. Of course, there was Spence, but he couldn't be a bridesmaid, although he would probably look good in a dress. My other close friends that have known me for years, I kept saying should I, shouldn't I, but if I had to think about it maybe I already knew my answer. They were not constantly in my life, they seemed to disappear off the face of the earth when they got a boyfriend, but when we did catch up it was like we had never been apart.

I got some good advice once from someone at a wedding fayre: if you can't have all your friends as bridesmaids give them other jobs to do. Ask one to be your witness, one to do a reading, which I thought was a genius idea. When I met up with these friends and they asked who the bridesmaids were, I cringed and then thought, should I ask them.

I had five bridesmaids, three big and two little, but the rate they were going I was going to have five bridesmaids taller than me. Oh dear. I would need them to all wear flats. How was I going to stand out amongst them? Maybe I would have to put them in awful dresses after all.

They thought they were being helpful, sending me pics of dresses they liked. I did think I will put them in different style dresses but the same colour, as they were all unique, different shapes and sizes, and all had different styles. Shoes, it didn't matter really, but I thought they would need to wear flats as three were already taller than me and by the time of the wedding the two younger ones would be, too, and I didn't want to look like a dwarf in photos.

I kept saying we would meet up and go shopping, but whenever we would arrange anything my endo would flare up. I wanted to have a nice day out so they could try on different styles see what suited them, then probably end up looking online as it would be much cheaper.

Edward had already sorted his stag do out, everyone invited and, paying off the amount monthly. He was going to Edinburgh for four days staying in a luxury penthouse, going on a whisky tour and taking part in the Highland Games, and he didn't even have to pay anything as the groom went free. I had always wanted to go to Benidorm, have a spa day and then have two nights out, one where I used to live and one where I currently lived, but at this rate I wouldn't be having one.

I still needed to come up with a colour scheme as I was constantly changing my mind. Did all brides do this? I needed to decide and stick to it, no going back. I did this, though, when we had our engagement party decided on the decorations in the venue when it was so dark that you couldn't see them anyway, and I ended up paying a lot more for gold and black decorations, plates, cutlery when I didn't even like it. So, lesson learnt from that, I think. I think I have answered my own question.

October

Another month gone. This was the second open evening wedding event at our venue I had been too since booking. This time I wasn't going to be distracted by free cake, prosecco, honeymoons or photographers, I was on a mission. I had written a list of things I wanted to do. I was going to take my tape measure to measure up as I would like to have bunting hung around the reception room but don't know what length I would need. I also wanted to time myself from entering the room to reaching the end of the aisle, as we still hadn't decided on a song yet, as our song that meant something to us seemed to be everybody's bloody wedding song lately. I knew it shouldn't matter, it was what we wanted, but I wanted to change it and had whittled it down to three, which was a start.

It was October and yet again I changed my bloody mind about centre pieces. These centre pieces would be the death of me. Fake flowers were the way I was going, definitely, but what to do with them, fuck only knows. I wanted fishbowls with floating sunflower heads, but I realised it wouldn't be the same with fake flowers, so that was off. Then I was thinking just to use jam jars or empty tins and place the flowers in them. I would just need to cover stems if in jars. Or I could put them in sand, would that be good to weigh them down too? The other idea was to have log slices with three jars and tealights all around. They actually had a table set up like that at our venue and it looked pretty and Edward liked it too. We sat down at the table to get a feel for whether guests would be able to see each other on the round tables and the centrepiece was the perfect height. We knew it would need to either be very tall or low, so this worked well. Had I finally decided? Log slices and jars, it was a lot less common than fishbowls, anyway.

Debbie had been pissing me off, too. She had been really distant and not bothered with me. I didn't know what her problem was but when I asked her, she said she was fine. You know that everything is not fine when someone says that. I should have been used to it by then as she had always been like it. I tried speaking to Edward about her but he just said, "I don't know why you bother with her, and he was right. She was the most two-faced person ever. She was always slagging off her close friends to me, but then the next thing you know she was saying how wonderful they were on social media and I thought, you have got to be fucking kidding me, right. It had made me think about her in a different way I did wonder if she was slagging off me to them too. When I texted her, when she eventually replied the conversation was cut short. It was like she didn't want to talk to me. Maybe she had got stuff going on, who knows. I knew there were a lot of people who suffered in silence me included, could be why she blew hot and cold all of the time. I was beginning to wish that I had never asked her to be my bloody bridesmaid, with her fake blonde hair and boobs. I knew my dad might have been pissed off, but I could just imagine her sour face in the photos with her overloaded, filled lips. Her moaning about her hair, the dress, the food; she was so high maintenance.

I had arranged a meal for close friends, bridesmaids and close family on both mine and Edward's sides, just women, so we could talk about the hen do, bridesmaid's dresses etcetera. no men allowed. When me, Chynna, and Debbie walked in, I could see her beady eyes scoping the place out immediately, she even picked up a wine glass as we were shown to our table to inspect for water marks. Debbie had only met my friends at family parties, but not when we were sober, sitting down for a meal.

When the waiter came over to take our drinks order, she spoke to him so slowly, like he was stupid and incapable of taking an order, that I knew he would probably spit in our food. I had tried to explain this to her, and you would have thought she would listen, but no, of course she wouldn't. When the waiter brought the drinks over, she said loudly, "Finally." He heard and I found myself mouthing the word sorry to him. I wanted the ground to open up, embarrassed was an underestimate, and the mood on the table was pretty much the same.

Debbie had ordered a red wine and started acting like she was wine tasting, smelling it and swishing it around in the glass. She then took a sip and just nodded and put it back down on the table. We were at the equivalent of a pub chain where you can get two meals for a tenner, not the Ritz. It was at this moment my mum let out the loudest fart you had ever heard. The waiter was so shocked he knocked the glass of red wine all over Debbie and of course she would be wearing a white floral top to make matters worse. She was mortified, lost for words I could see that she was about to blow when Jodie piped up, "You know the best thing for getting red wine out?" She then threw her glass of white wine at Debbie, but instead of going in the same place as the red wine, it got her in the face. She stormed out and everyone just fell about laughing. My mum was mortified as she thought the fart was going to be a silent one. I ran after Debbie but she was too angry to speak, so thought best to leave her be. This night had been ruined, was supposed to be all about me, and now it had become about her, even with her not being the she was still the main topic of conversation.

The next day I felt down and even cried. I had been awake half the night as we had a storm and the wind whistling was doing my head in. I'm surprised it had kept me up, the amount of drinks I mixed. But no, wide awake, lying there with the room spinning. The thought of a drink now literally made me heave. Debbie hadn't returned any messages I had sent her and I had the worst hangover in history. It was eight-thirty in the morning and I had already puked six times. The only time my head would not pound was when I was laying down with my arm pressed firmly against it in front of an open window, with the cold air hitting my face. The mixture of prosecco, whiskey, beer and tequila was not the greatest idea I blame Chynna, it was the shots that done it, I'm sure, and they were always her idea. When I looked out of the window, when I could eventually stand up without running to the loo to be sick, our fence had blown down. Great. Well, they say things come in threes: the same day our oven and kettle decided to pack up too.

I was definitely feeling sorry for myself that is why I was crying. It has dawned on me that we had eleven months to pay for everything. We had no spare cash lying around and we are saving as much as we could as it was. Please would someone just give us a fucking break. I called Spence and he was no help. He just said to postpone it. I think people forgot that this was our wedding. If it was theirs, I wouldn't dream about being unenthusiastic about what they wanted. I would be a friend and do everything I could to help, whether I liked their ideas or not. Don't get me wrong, Chynna, Jodie, my brothers and both sets of parents had been amazing and supportive. Why couldn't everyone be? But at the end of the day, it was our wedding, we had to pay for it.

Sure, we were getting help, which we were extremely grateful for, but we still had to put in a large chunk. It was harder when work had become more demanding too and I dreaded going in. I didn't know how I got through the day at that moment when you have nothing to look forward to but a wedding in a year's time, which I know is a big thing to be happy about, but at what cost? No holidays or breaks, barely see my fiancé as he works overtime all the time to pay for this wedding, and Malcolm constantly in the back of my head. Why did memories of him keep coming back to me clearer and more frequent? I needed to talk to someone about it as it was beginning to drive me crazy, needed to get these thoughts out of my head. I needed my mum.

November

I had arrived at mum's house. I don't remember the journey as I had done it so many times before. I sat in the car outside for what seemed like hours, when it was literally minutes. Thinking about Malcolm and all the other men in my past. What was it about me, did I do something? From Uncle M's kisses to Malcolm, to a family friend who was kind to me and always paid me compliments, but when his wife was out of the room would touch my boobs. One of my auntie's boyfriends would stare at me and stick his tongue out suggestively in a sexual way and try and get my attention when no one was looking by whispering dirty things to me. I was doubting myself again. Was it me after all? Was I just taking it the wrong way? Maybe it wasn't sexual and it was me over thinking again. I was about to drive away but then I saw my mum peeking through the blinds. Pushing the window in the front room open she shouted, "Hello, love, give me a minute."

Okay this was it; I was going to finally tell my mum what had happened to me all those years ago it was now or never. Maybe telling her the truth would help me to deal with the abuse, as I had felt tremendous guilt for not being able to talk to her about it all these years. But she had been ill, suffering with depression, during that time and it would have broken her if she knew. She was in a much better place now. I felt that Malcolm was weighing heavier on my mind lately, don't get me wrong, he was always there in the background however much I tried to ignore him, eating away at my personality. He had changed me from the person I once was and thought one day I may become.

I was deep in thought, thinking about other victims of abuse and why their harrowing stories would come out years later, usually when the abuser in question was dead. A couple of celebrities sprung to mind. Only people who have been through it would understand. It's not that you can just come out with 'hey, guess what I was abused', although it would have been easier if you could. He was the reason I had no confidence and why I never had the courage to tell Spence how I felt as he made me feel not good enough. I think the reason I had never settled down before was because the men I was attracted to were always the wrong ones. All they would want to do was change me or control me by telling me what to wear, or not to wear make-up because I was much prettier without it. That was a lie if ever I heard one. Who looks better without make up? It would always be lovely in the start. They would treat me well, pay me compliments, but then a few months down the line they would change, but did this happen to every man in a relationship? Would this eventually happen with Edward and me?

There were so many times before when I wanted to tell my mum, but my head stopped me from doing so.

When she eventually opened the front door, I immediately stepped back from the outstretched arms coming in for a hug. She was a huggy person. I followed her in and sat down in the front room looking at photos of me and my siblings as children. Me all smart in my suits.

Mum put the kettle on and shouted from the kitchen, "How many sugars?"

"'None, Mum." I hadn't had sugar in my tea for about fifteen years but still my mum asked me every time and still managed to put a sugar in there, even though I would say I didn't have any.

Handing me the tea, Mum sat opposite me. She had been decorating again, looked like Moroccan style this time, from the red feature wall, fringed patterned throws and cushions. My mum had named me India as she had always wanted to go there. She would have trinkets, sandalwood incense burning and wear bangles, and have Indian elephants dotted around the place. It looked like a shrine to Ganesh by the time I got older, but then she would get bored and decide on somewhere else she wanted to go. China was the theme when my sister was born. I am glad I wasn't born now as I could have been called Morocco.

"Biscuit? I've got them ones you like, the nobby ones?" She got out of her seat again.

"Please, Mum, just sit down. I need to talk to you."

My mum then got up again and grabbed the biscuits from the kitchen cupboard.

"Please just *sit down*, Mum. I don't want a biscuit. I just want you to listen." I wouldn't have been able to stomach it usually but the sugary tea was surprisingly good. They do say it's good for shock a sugar in your tea.

Mum was about to start talking again when I put my hand up to say stop.

I had to interrupt her otherwise I would have been there all night whilst she moaned about work or other members of the family.

"Listen! It's about Malcolm."

Mum looked shocked and went to the sink fiddling with the taps to avoid looking at me.

"You know, the guy who moved into that house on Blackburn Road after he renovated it. I used to go round there. He used to come round here for coffee."

"I know who he is, India."

The colour started draining from her face.

"Mum, you okay?"

"Yes, love, just give me a minute," she replied, running to the toilet.

When the hurling stopped, she reappeared.

She had been wanting to tell me for so long the truth, why she divorced and why I was treated differently to my siblings.

She looked up into my eyes, mascara running down her face placed her hand on mine and said, "You have figured it out, haven't you, love?"

Now I was confused.

"There was never going to be a right time to tell you this, India, but now is as good as time as any. Malcolm was your father."

1983

My mum had met Malcolm in summer 1983. She was temping in an office at the time for a building firm in West London where we used to live up until I was one. It was there she had met him, all dirty from a day's work labouring and had popped in the office to see what other work he had on that week as was passing in his van. He was a right Delboy, had the gift of the gab and was also very charming and attractive, despite wearing dusty clothes and having a face that needed a good wash. His curly hair which was dark brown looked whiter with the amount of paint in it and he had beautiful almond shaped brown eyes. He left her with a smile on her face and she hoped he would call in again as he made her day when he would come in. His visits to the office became more regular and she wondered if the reason was her as he could have got the information he needed over the phone. But he would always say it was quicker to pop in, or he was passing by.

Marie had never felt good enough or appreciated by her husband. They had married young. He would work all day and come home and just expect his dinner on the table and then just sit in front of the TV all evening. At twenty-four, she fell pregnant and she was so happy, but

Ken didn't seem excited at all. He didn't want to tell anyone so she felt she couldn't be happy about it or get excited. This amazing time in her life had been made horrible, like she wasn't allowed to talk about it, or even mention anything to do with the baby.

The moment she saw the blood on wiping when she went to the toilet, she knew she was miscarrying. It was like she was waiting for it as every time she went to the toilet she would check for blood and be relieved when there was not any. Maybe Ken was right after all. My mum still got upset years later when she saw pregnancy announcements before twelve weeks, because you never know what could happen, and up until that first scan you had a high chance of miscarriage. Maybe she just thought like this because she'd had a miscarriage, as when she found out she was pregnant all she wanted to do was tell people, make plans and buy baby bits. But Ken stopped her and he was right. How would she have felt telling people she was pregnant and then having to tell them she had lost it? You would have thought this would have brought them closer together, but it did the complete opposite as she was devasted and he seemed to not give a shit. She would cry all the time about it. After all, she had lost a life that had been growing inside her, but he would say it's only an embryo, not like it was a baby yet. But it was to her and she did not want to just forget about it. She had worked out the due date and was thinking about names and schools. But everyone dealt with grief differently I guess maybe that was his way.

It was her Christmas office party Marie hadn't drunk for what seemed like forever as she had been pregnant and then in pain for a couple of weeks and in too much of an emotional state after the miscarriage, so that night she dolled herself up in a black velvet off the shoulder dress which hugged her curves, did her makeup and had her hair permed, and she thought she looked quite attractive for once. The party was in full swing. She started with Bacardi and coke, then went onto gin and bitter lemon. Funny how drinks go in and out of fashion, as you don't hear anyone drinking Bacardi any more but gin is the in thing now. You can get every flavour under the sun.

Feeling confident, she strutted her stuff on the dancefloor—well, a corner of the office that didn't have desks or chairs in the way—and stumbled, perhaps due to her patent neon stilettos that she wasn't use to wearing, or because of all the gin. Malcolm steadied her and she leaned in for a cuddle. She wanted to feel something again, needed some comfort. Ken hadn't been giving her any, barely touched her any more. She had to remind him to kiss her before he left for work. The rest of the night was a bit of a blur.

She woke up in her bed, still dressed. She did not have any knickers on and when she felt down below, she knew she'd had sex, just couldn't remember it, but Ken was lying next to her. Thank fuck for that, she thought.

Two weeks later she started to feel rough, sick and had sore boobs like she was going to come on. She thought she would go to the doctors as something was definitely wrong and he confirmed she was pregnant.

She named me India after her love for the country, although she had never been. I had big brown eyes and lots of dark hair and from the moment she saw me all covered in white mucky stuff, she was in love. She could not believe that she had created such perfection and was amazed about how I had been inside her for all that time. Although looking down at her bump, it still looked like the baby was in there as it did not seem to go down at all afterwards; she wondered if she had another one still in there. Everything was great apart from she was barely sleeping, looked like a tramp and could not remember the last time she had brushed her teeth or eaten, but she had the most perfect little baby, so none of that mattered. It brought her and Ken closer together. He was a brilliant dad and doted on me.

A couple of weeks after being back at work after having nearly nine months off, Malcolm came into the office.

'Long time no see,' he said.

Marie smiled. She had not seen him since the Christmas party. 'Yeah, it has. How you been?' she replied.

'Good, actually, I have been waiting to see you. I have something of yours in the van.'

'For me?' Her face dropped when she saw him walking back with a small carrier bag. As she opened it, inside, she saw her knickers.

'I think these belong to you,' he whispered with a wink.

She felt sick to the stomach. Did she have sex with him that night? Was he India's father? What if he wanted custody? Would she have to tell him? She kept picturing India's beautiful face and she could see the resemblance now. She didn't look like Ken at all; the dark features came from Malcolm. Her little family bubble that she had been in would now be burst. He would put two and two together if he found out she had a nine-month-old. It would not take a rocket scientist, would it. She wished she could remember that night; she blamed the fucking gin.

Talk about beating me to it with the bad news. I couldn't tell her now that he had sexually abused me, could I? Finding out my dad was not my real dad and my real dad was my childhood abuser, how could they have lied to me for my whole life?

So, as you have probably guessed, I was stressed out. The wedding was the last thing on my mind at the moment but we were running out of time we only had ten months left my anxiety had peaked. Maybe the answer was to cancel it with everything that's going on?

Uncle M's face became clearer to me now too; it was Malcolm who would visit my mum and it must have been to see me, his child. They were the same person; how did I not realise this before.

It's funny how things come back to you, as I must have blocked it out, he would often visit when my dad was at work or Mum would take me to the park and he would meet us there. It was Mum who called him Uncle M but said to keep it a secret from my dad and I did, as he would treat me to anything I wanted. So I learnt how to lie from a young age. Something I had mastered over the years.

Dad said they were trying to protect me and didn't want me to feel left out. The reason they had divorced too was because my dad thought Mum was having an affair and had confronted her one evening and she confessed all. I can remember that night I had woken from a reoccurring dream I used to have where I was being chased up a tall tower with a winding staircase, with one window at the top, and the only way to get away was to jump off. I would always wake up scared before I jumped. I was standing by the living room door which they used to shut so they could have the TV on and it wouldn't wake any of us kids up. I overheard one night Mum say I wasn't his. I didn't know what she meant at the time. Now I do.

It all finally made sense. The expensive clothes; my mum had not bought them at all. I knew she could never had afforded them; she only worked part time in an office. My mum going into a state of depression after finding out someone had accused him of sexual assault.

Why didn't I figure this out sooner all the signs were there? The cuddle the first time me and Malcolm were alone? Why I looked differently from my other siblings, just thought I was a throwback, it can happen. The person I had thought was my dad for my whole life was not the person I thought he was at all. Standing in my mum's hallway, looking in the Moroccan inspired mirror that I had loved as it was so detailed and ornate, but today I hated it as when I looked at my reflection, I just wanted to claw my face off—all I could see was his face. How could Malcolm be my father and my abuser? Did he know? He must have done, all the visits to mum and the clothes that she clearly could not afford, the same designer gear he would wear, even when he was working—they must have been from him. And even moving down the same road as her, that wouldn't have been a coincidence.

He always used to compliment me on my clothes, too. I felt sick to the stomach. Now I knew why; that was because he had bloody bought them. Why didn't my mum tell me sooner? I felt so angry, punching the wall so hard that it made my knuckles bleed. The anger I felt then turned to tears. I needed a fag or to jump off the nearest building, either or would suffice at this precise moment.

The thought that my own father had touched me in a sexual way and took away my virginity was sick. He was sick. I had his genes; did that mean that being an abuser could be hereditary? I thought back to that night and how, after it happened, I just walked the streets before heading home and stood in the back garden looking at the swing and playhouse one of Mum's blokes had built for us, knowing I was no longer a child. He had the cheek to be round my house when I got home, knowing that if he got there first then I would not be able to tell my mum what had happened. Was that why I kept going back, because deep down I felt a connection? I had always questioned why I kept going back after the first time he put his fingertips inside my knickers. Did I know subconsciously that he was my father, so thought it was okay? Was it even abuse at all or his way of showing love? Your dad was allowed to look at your vagina, wasn't he? But up until what age was that acceptable, I thought. It was different with my mum; she saw me naked all the time and I wouldn't think twice about getting changed in front of her.

I thought back to the police interview room and how if I had just told the truth then, maybe I would have found out sooner that he was my dad. I had never been to a police station before, let alone interviewed, I knew it was about Malcolm as other children from the street had been called in including Spence so was expecting to be called. But it wasn't how I imagined. It was more like a hospital waiting room, if you went private. Cosy chairs and carpeted floors. A coffee machine in the corner. A box of tissues on the table that sat in the middle of the chairs, with a vase of fresh flowers. Just a few small windows high up that you could not see out of as the glass was frosted and way too high, unless you stood on a chair, but let in just enough natural light for the light not to be turned on. But I was a child, after all, so maybe this was a special room just for kids. The policewoman wasn't in uniform either. She wore an oversized shirt and jeans with a flowery scarf and looked more like my art teacher, but she made me feel comfortable from the start. She told me she liked my shoes, they were another present from my mum black patent with a chunky Perspex heel. That way you open up, I suppose, but I still lied my arse off. My mum had not been well since the accusations about Malcolm had come out. Someone sprayed pedo on his front door, too which had upset my mum. She even helped him clean it off, marching round there she went with her rubber gloves, bucket and scouring pad. My mum was in a particularly bad way after that. She had episodes like this before and battled with depression, but I had never seen her this bad. She would be tearful one minute and would not come out of her bedroom, and the next minute she would be going mental and smashing plates in the kitchen. She did take medication for it but, in my opinion, she needed a higher dose or something different, as clearly it was not working. She scared me sometimes as her behaviour would be so unpredictable. I wouldn't know who I was coming home too but I tried to shield my brothers and sister from it as much as I could.

The only thing I told the nice policewoman was that he'd hugged me once; which was not a lie I just left out all of the other things he had done. I knew mum was watching the footage from another room as there was a small camera pointed directly towards me recording every word I said.

Edward was away again another training course, which did not help as I was home alone with my thoughts, which was definitely not a good thing. I couldn't sleep and would lay awake overthinking everything. Trying to figure out what I was going to do next. I couldn't get Malcolm out of my head. I didn't even know if I wanted to be around any more. Sure, there had been times in my life before when I had wanted to end it all. Hasn't everyone?

Edward was rarely at home any more so didn't notice anything was different with me. I even started smoking again since the dad news, but in secret, so no one else knew. I became a master at hiding the cigarettes. I would put them inside a paracetamol box in my bag, so if Edward went in there for any reason, he wouldn't find them unless he had a headache. I made any excuse when Edward was at home to go to the shop just so I could nip out for a fag. You would think I would have smelt of smoke but he never said anything.

The first fag after three years was vile as I breathed in; it burned the back of my throat like it had when I first took a cigarette down as a teenager. Before then I would pretend to try and act cool and would just hold the smoke in my mouth then blow it out. When I did take it down, I coughed my bloody guts up, but after that it was okay I got the knack. It left the most awful taste in my mouth, but by the third one it was good again.

Edward had been more distant with me, not interested in what I had to say, constantly on his phone and always would rather be out than spending time with me when I needed him the most. He didn't even want to have sex any more would always make an excuse, or make sure he went to bed after me when I was already asleep, gone were the days of him bending me over the sofa during dinner. He was suddenly into losing weight and watching what he ate. He was even dressing differently and had been going to the barbers to get his short hair, cut rather than doing it himself with his clippers. I had noticed, too, that he has been liking a lot of girls' selfies on social media. Maybe he knew them, I don't know. It had crossed my mind that he could be having an affair; to be honest who could blame him, life was stressful at the moment. He wasn't that private about his phone, though, leaving it lying around. If he was having an affair would he do that? Or did he know that I wasn't the type of girl to go through his phone? I had never done that in the past and would not now because I trusted him.

He was constantly doing overtime, so I didn't see him that often due to our shifts clashing and it felt like he would rather be at work than at home with me. Well, that's how I felt anyway. I had tried to talk to him about it, but he just said that he was doing the overtime for me. For our wedding. But I was like what wedding, there won't be one as I don't see you enough. There was once a time when he would rush home to see me as he missed me. But that had changed over the last few months. I was always at home lately as I didn't really want to see anybody, but he was still going out and seeing friends, when all I wanted was for him to be there with me or take me out. I felt isolated and alone sometimes, but I knew a lot of it was my own doing. Maybe it would be better if he was having an affair, who would want to be stuck with me anyway.

We argued now over stupid things. I was also moody a lot of the time, which I think then put him in a mood, but I couldn't help it. In previous relationships I had been a quiet little mouse, didn't dare to answer back, never argued; just accepted everything the other person said and apologised, even if it wasn't my fault, but that got me nowhere. This relationship was different. If I disagreed with something, I would say it, hence why we argue, but I think it is healthy to argue a bit, isn't it? Edward definitely bought out my fiery side.

Going back to the whole affair thing, I felt like he wasn't there for me any more. He constantly disagreed with every word I said. if I said the sky was blue, he would say it wasn't. Could he be seeing someone at work? He was doing all of this overtime.

That's how we met, through work. I knew of him to say hi to but thought he was a bit of an arsehole, thought a bit highly of himself. I did fancy him but didn't think he would ever look twice at me. It just so happened that one day I had taken patients for so many X-rays that we got to talking. He was not like I thought at all. He was ambitious, kind, funny and just so easy to talk to. I felt like I had known him years and for the first time ever I did not want to leave work, as I wanted to still talk to him. That shift changed everything for me. That's what made me scared. What if the same thing had happened with someone else? Maybe he was just trying to find the right time to tell me. Do I just ask him?

I wasn't enjoying life at that moment. There was a time when I could tell Edward anything, but lately things had changed. I had been scared to speak to him as I didn't know how he would react.

Spence was there for me yet again to cry on his shoulder and comfort me by holding me close and kissing me again on the head, as he had been all them years before, after I told him about Malcolm; he didn't judge me and had been the only one really there for me lately as couldn't speak to mum and dad could I? Was I doing the right thing marrying Edward? Was he the one I should be with? Spence made me feel alive and had been there for me when I needed someone the most. He always seemed to be there. Lately Edward had been distracted and I felt he had gone off me. Anyway, so what if he was having an affair and would leave me eventually anyway?

Was I meant to be with Spence instead?

Maybe it was just doubt. Did everyone go through this, thinking maybe we weren't meant to be together. Were we supposed to get married? This was for life. I wanted him to be my first and only husband, so it needed to be right. Lately it had become apparent how different we were, and would this get harder if we decide to have children? Who knows?

I knew I couldn't carry on like this as I would have ended up having a breakdown, as I felt the lowest that I ever had. So, I just asked Edward outright at breakfast one morning about how he was feeling about us and if he did still want to marry me. I had to know as I had so much going on in my head. I was waiting for him to say he had met someone else or that he didn't want to be with me any more but he said the opposite to my surprise. If only I had spoken to him sooner and didn't just assume how he was feeling by his actions. He said he didn't want me to have to be under any more stress than I already was.

The new healthy lifestyle is so he looked good for when we got married and he was in a healthier place for if we did have children and all of the overtime and the extra training was to be able to earn more money to pay for the wedding.

I felt so bad that I had doubted him and wished I had confronted him sooner. Why did I always think the worst of men? Probably due to the fact that my dad had lied to me for twenty-eight years and my real dad was a paedophile. I needed to stop letting men from my past affect my future, I put Spence to the back of my mind.

He did still want to get married but we were going through so much then that he thought it best to take one thing at a time. He said it didn't matter when we got married, but we needed to do what was best for us and he wished I would just talk to him more rather than letting things build up and then, over something stupid like running out of toilet roll, it became a massive argument. Being open and honest with each other and making time for each other had made such a difference. I felt so much happier in myself.

We had already pretty much sorted out everything for our traditional wedding and it was now less than ten months away. I had a dream wedding all booked, just needing to be paid for. But something Edward said has stayed with me and was so true. It didn't matter when we got married or where; we needed to do what was best for us. He wanted me to be honest with him if something was bothering me. I told him about me smoking and he felt bad that I felt I hide to hide it from him. I told him everything about the last few weeks since finding out about my dad and even said I felt like I didn't want to be here any more. It was like we were after we first met, he was so lovely and supportive then and he was exactly the same now.

Edward was only was doing the whole big wedding for me anyway. My immediate family had been so excited, counting down the days. I just felt that if we decided to take the leap and bugger off, we were going to be letting so many people down. But at the end of the day, it was our wedding. Did we just go through with all of our plans and make everyone else happy or should we actually do what we wanted to do?

I read something that day that said: "Don't feel bad for making decisions that upset other people. You're not responsible for their happiness, you're responsible for yours". I must have read that a hundred times. My whole life I had done what other people wanted me to do. I never wanted to upset anyone and just did things to please other people, but then what happens is people walk all over you. For the first time, I could actually do something that I wanted for a change.

For the last three days Edward had been asking me if I had made my mind up. Like it was that simple. I couldn't think clearly; my head was like scrambled egg. He couldn't understand what the big deal was. Men totally think differently to women. He would just say forget about it, there is nothing you can do now. You will be talking to your mum and dad soon, so what's the big deal. If it was only that, that had been playing on my mind. I thought he understood. But the last few days he had gone back to how he was being before I confided in him again. When I first told him about the abuse, he was so understanding, but was that because it was new in our relationship and nothing the other person says really bothers you as you are newly in love and love is blind. He had changed so much, I didn't even know if marrying him at all was the right thing to do any more my earlier doubts reappeared again, as he was not there when I needed him the most. He even gave me a deadline until the end of the month to make a firm decision. If you don't know me by now, I left it, of course, until the last minute, until D-day. In my head I had planned what I was going to do but these thoughts were not put into action. This is the story of my life lol. I thought the best thing to do would be to talk to my mum and dad first and see what their thoughts were on the whole idea, but it was hard. Due to what had happened our relationship wasn't the same; although I was finally speaking to them again, it was hard not to without telling everyone else the truth and I didn't want everyone to know as this would be the talk of the town. At this rate there would not even be a wedding as we may have even split up before then due to stress. This had caused so much tension between us. I only planned to get married once, but I suppose every bride said that. You do not get married to think that you will get divorced one day.

With ten months to go we had decided to cancel the wedding. You would think I would be happier that at least that was one less thing to think about, but maybe having to focus was keeping me sane.

I am not going to lie; with everything going on it had caused a massive strain on mine and Edward's relationship. Things had been great for a couple of weeks after our talk we went back to how things use to be having sex every night but now things had gone back to how they were before but I thought it must be me. I was hard to live with and everything he seemed to do or didn't do would irritate me and, instead of letting it go, I had to make a massive deal about it which then ended up in an argument. I even said that I had changed my mind about the wedding, to just to cancel it full stop. Of course, I didn't mean it. I was frustrated not just sexually. He was the closest person to me, so I was taking everything out on him, as I still didn't know if we had made the right decision. Yes, we would be saving money but at what cost. We bickered constantly. I kept having doubts in my head, too, that I had made the wrong decision. Should we even be getting married if we had such different outlooks on things? He seemed to be carrying on like it was not a big deal, but it was.

Our wedding was cancelled. We just needed to start letting everyone know now.

So, venue cancelled, registrar cancelled, photographer cancelled; that was the three main things done. Things were in motion, no changing our minds now as deposits had been lost. I still hadn't told everybody yet. I told my immediate family and close friends. Spencer was shocked when I told him and thought we had split up, but when I explained he was actually really supportive and even offered to help out with the cost. He had sure changed his tune all of a sudden.

We hadn't booked anything else yet, but we needed to get a wriggle on really, I still needed to arrange holiday and cancel the time I'd originally booked off in September, but firstly I thought we needed to tell everyone else we had invited. Edward was so laid back about it, but I definitely wasn't. Maybe we needed to book abroad and sort out the date of the party, so we could say to people we have cancelled this wedding but you are invited to the party instead on such and such a date. I thought I would sell my wedding dress too as Edward would need to help me into it, so it wouldn't have the same reaction, plus it was a bit dramatic for Vegas, if that was where we went and I didn't fancy lugging that through the airport as it would not fit in a suitcase and I would have to take it as carry on. I felt a bit numb about it all, like it hadn't sunk in yet.

The responses I had got so far when we cancelled the venue etcetera had been very empathetic, which I was surprised about, but actually this was quite a big thing to decide, I suppose, and not a decision that had been made lightly. It was funny how many people actually knew we were getting married in September, as for the next few weeks I constantly had people saying not long to go until the big day. I had actually found it hilarious telling them it had been cancelled and seeing their shocked faces and them not knowing what to say. I had been cruel and left it a little while before saying that we were still getting married, we were not just not doing the whole big British wedding thing; now we were going to do it for ourselves.

January and February

January was nearing its end and my new year's resolution was to communicate more about how I felt.

We were still no further forward with a decision as to what we are going to do. But what would be would be. What was the right thing to do? If I had a pound for every time a family member asked any more news, I think I would have been able to pay off the original planned wedding. I still hadn't decided whether to sell my dress. When I spoke to Edward about it he said don't do it yet, just in case we get married here. Not knowing if I would be wearing my dress? Should I just sell it now? I know there was so much going on now that it was difficult to set a date again. It was a new year. I thought this would be a better year, but it started shit, to say the least. When the clock struck midnight and fireworks were going off in the neighbourhood, I thought this was going to be our year.

I spoke too soon. Every day lately there seemed to be a story on the news about someone who was killed tragically or died suddenly for no apparent reason and you thought it was sad and felt so sorry for the family and friends they had left behind, but because you didn't know the person they seemed so far away that you never thought it would happen to you. In January reality had hit me that things do happen to people you care about, as my dad had a huge lump come up on his face, it had been there a while but was not as noticeable as it was now. The next few weeks he was in and out of hospital. He even was talking about his funeral plans and what songs he wanted played.

For the first time in my life, I realised that my parents wouldn't be around forever, and this scared the shit out of me.

Luckily my dad was okay and after numerous tests and surgery they removed a tumour which thankfully was benign. But this may have not been the case. This brought me and mum closer again as although she and my dad were no longer together, she still cared for him. We were a family and they stick together and I needed my mum and dad more than ever now.

I knew me and Edward needed to make a decision, I wanted my mum and dad to see me married and settled I needed some happy news as all this year so far had been doom and gloom; life was way too short and I'd only just realised.

So…we are getting married in seven weeks' time. Yep, I know literally made the decision overnight. I had just been casually looking at holidays to Vegas as we had a week off in April, so I just asked Edward outright, how about getting married then? To get married in this country it was a bit of a palaver. You had to find a register office, give at least twenty-eight days' notice, and also book an appointment to give notice of marriage with identification. We thought this would be cutting it a bit fine here as we still would have to find a venue at this short notice, so abroad would need to be the way forward. We could actually go to Vegas for five nights for a reasonable amount of money a lot cheaper than having a wedding here? Also, we could have five whole days of fun, rather than one long day that goes by in a flash. Of course, the downside was short notice, so it would only be us that could go, but I would rather all or nothing and at the end of the day it was just going to be about the two of us. So now seven weeks away; a lot can happen in a few months.

We booked upgraded flights—it was our wedding after all—and five-star luxury in a suite. Again, it was our wedding and probably our honeymoon, as I couldn't see us going on one of those anytime soon.

The next thing was to tell the family. I called my mum and dad and they were actually over the moon, really pleased. My sister and brothers were excited too. Next thing was to tell Edward's parents; this was what I was dreading the most as since we had cancelled the previous wedding, they would keep asking about what was going on. But Edward just came straight out and told them and they were overjoyed. I think looking back they just wanted us to get married for us; they were not pressurizing us. I finally felt I could get excited. Everyone close knew, friends would be fine, bridesmaids maybe not but you can't please everyone, now we could start planning wedding number two. So, all systems go, go, go.

Why do people just assume that if you get married in Vegas Elvis is going to be involved in some way shape or form? Actually, going back to before we booked anything many months ago, that was my exact image. Too funny how you just associate certain things with certain places.

With only seven weeks to go. I decided I needed to start bridal preparations. First things first, start eating better and hopefully lose a few pounds, a course of sunbeds as I wanted to look healthy. I don't do fake tan after an incident where I ended up streaky and orange, and looking like an oompa loompa. Plus, I didn't want to stain the dress with it on the day, as I have had a few mishaps with tan sweating onto my clothes before and according to the forecast the weather was in the upper twenties in April. I was a bit concerned about the sunbeds, though, as I'd had a bad experience when I was seventeen.

I worked as a retail assistant in a fashion clothes store and every couple of days my colleagues would go for a sunbed; it was something that they all did. Stand up sunbeds were very popular, so I started going to fit in, although I am quite tanned as I naturally had olive skin. Everything was going great until one day I went, decided to go on for nine minutes instead of my usual six. I remember feeling so hot in there that day, I know it's supposed to be hot but a lot hotter. An intense warm sensation came over me quickly spreading from my face to my body I felt like my insides were cooking or on fire. This is what it must have felt like to be cooked in a microwave. I had to get out of there. I was sweating way more than I should have been and couldn't catch my breath. As soon as I got out into the fresh air I collapsed on the floor and my vision had gone blurry and I couldn't hear again. It brought me back to the time I had my tattoo as I had exactly the same reaction. Luckily a passer-by stopped to check if I was all right, bought me a bottle of water and sat on the floor with me until I felt better. It didn't take long, thank god. I wanted the ground to open up and swallow me. So, as you can imagine I hadn't stepped foot in a sunbed shop since, so I was a bit dubious. But beauty is pain, wedding pictures would be around forever. I would just make sure that I didn't go alone and maybe start with six minutes and work my way up gradually, and avoid stand-ups; lay-downs would be the way forward.

March Hen Do

So originally, when we had a year to go, I wanted to go to Benidorm in Spain: sun, sea, and sand, over a hundred disco bars the last time I checked, and a vibrant nightlife, the perfect place for a hen do. Somewhere there were karaoke bars as I did love a bit of a sing song. The weather was usually hot enough to get a tan most months of the year and we would be looking to go summer time. Not a long flight, about two hours forty-five minutes from London and pretty cheap, but obviously this was not going to happen now. At the girlie meal we had in October, nothing ended up getting sorted out in the end due to what happened with Debbie we just ended up getting drunk. My bridesmaids had arranged a couple of other dates since for us to get together have a few drinks and discuss hen do options and get plans in motion, but on both occasions on arranging this I had to cancel due to my endometriosis pain flaring and leaving me bed bound. We did set up a group chat and had even decided on a date for when we would do it. We thought a month before the big day, as it left a long time to get over a hangover and start detoxing before the big day and also, if we did go abroad, dodgy tan lines would fade.

I couldn't expect friends and family to pay to go abroad when we only had seven weeks until the wedding, so decided to have a lower key one instead. I have always celebrated St Patrick's Day. I am not Irish at all, and I hate the taste of Guinness, although I did have it once with champagne which was good, black velvet, I think it's called. But I love it, leprechauns and Guinness hats. I have always had a good night, so when better to have my hen do and this year it fell on a Saturday, even better. Now traditionally isn't it your maid of honour who sorts out the hen do? Well, this was my sister and she was more than happy to be in charge. The problem was with me; who would I invite? We would need to go somewhere where the older ladies could sit down, not somewhere too rowdy, and a starting point for everyone to meet. Cheap drink was a must also. It would be nice to sip cocktails the price of two packets of fags, but I wasn't really that kind of girl, as much I would like to be, but I hadn't got the budget, although I would like nice toilets.

Inviting women to the hen do was as hard as inviting people to the wedding. Who do you invite? It was stressing me out and I hadn't got the time to sit there and think about it. I needed to give notice to people otherwise it would end up with being just me and my sister, although we would still have a good time. So, the first thing was family. Hindsight says I should have invited all my aunties, cousins etcetera, regardless of who they were speaking to or had fallen out with, but I didn't. I decided to keep it low key and just invite family that were local as it was short notice and they wouldn't travel. Most of them didn't even turn up to our engagement party. Next stop, friends and work colleagues, and before I knew it I had twenty-five people on the list. I knew some wouldn't come as there were only three weeks before St Patrick's Day, but I was surprised how many people said yes. I did think in the back of my mind how many people would actually turn up, but I was pleased.

Then, should we have a theme, that was another thought? Dress up like leprechauns, wear something green or just look very tacky? I decided on none of these and decided venue again was key to start the night. I did initially want a meal first, but that would be added expense. I would have to pre-book, get deposits etcetera and I couldn't be bothered to sort it out, if I'm honest, so I had a look online and went around a few pubs, and in the end my sister found an Irish one. They said we could decorate an area and start the night there.

Then on to decorations. My sister had already bought a few, so I ordered a few more bits, banners saying hen party and inflatable warning sign and balloons, and also ordered sashes for everyone as my sister was putting together little bags for the hens with the must haves, like willy straws and dare cards.

A week to go everyone had been told the venue and start time. I had my decorating committee sorted and they had arrived. My sister was sorting out the goody bags, so all done. Only a couple of people couldn't make it due to prior commitments, so for once things were going my way.

I even had my outfit sorted finally after ordering about twenty different things online. I knew I should have just gone shopping but it's so much easier to order clothes online and you can get it the next day. No going out in the cold, driving around the town looking for parking. The only down side was sending the nineteen items back as I had to go to the post office for that.

Everything was going great until four days before the event. We had a weather warning for snow, would you believe it. This had happened a few years prior, snow in March, but I didn't think for one second, we would have it this year. I could hear my phone going off already, but actually I was surprised. Everyone just told me not to worry, it was only a warning and probably wouldn't hit us, and to only worry about it if it happened.

Guess what? It did happen, not as bad as the weather man said, but it had settled on the paths, although the roads were clear, and it was freezing like in the minuses. But the night went ahead as planned. A few people pulled out due to the weather and travelling in it, which was understandable as I wouldn't have driven in it. I had been driving for fourteen years and still haven't driven in snow. I would be a hazard to others I'm sure.

The morning of the hen do, me and Debbie arrived at the pub to decorate an area. The landlady didn't even remember me and the pub was packed, and it was only eleven-thirty in the morning. Some sporting event was on and there were no tables free. I couldn't believe it. I didn't even have a backup plan. We were carrying helium balloons, banners, inflatables, L-plates, with nowhere to put them. I cried, went outside and tried to think of a plan B, but Debbie just said let's just find a corner and get it done. It didn't matter that there were not any tables. There may be later. We just needed a starting area so went back in and found a corner that was unoccupied and started decorating.

I had never felt so embarrassed. not only was everyone staring at us, I couldn't even blow anything up. So glad I didn't get the "same penis forever balloons now". The clientele in there weren't a young crowd, but were very much middle aged and they all seemed to be judging us. It didn't help that the TV screen was right above us too, so they all had to look in our direction.

I am a planner. In my head, before my hen do, I thought of all the things I needed to do before the night beauty wise: sunbeds, waxing, hair and nails done, fake eyelashes; leaving enough time to get ready so not to rush and take time have a drink, but this didn't go to plan just like my engagement plan I will never learn. Me, Chynna, Debbie and a few close friends decided to stay in a hotel on the hen night, so we could get ready together and have breakfast in the morning plus they didn't live local. We decided on staying in the hotel where I was originally going to get married, so I would get a chance to stay there after all, and they had a good deal on that weekend for bed and breakfast So, the first thing that happened was me and Debbie turned up at the hotel and no one else was there great. I had asked when booking if all of the rooms could be together in the outside part of the hotel; that way we wouldn't have to walk through reception, pissed as farts, waking up all of the other guests. I thought this was the case but didn't check as when they gave me the key it was to one of the outside rooms, so I assumed they had answered my request. All checked in, I thought I know, I have hours before going out so I'll start doing my hair now.

So, there I was, I had curled half of my hair with the straighteners when Chynna called and said they were in the hotel bar. Great, half hair straight, half curly, but I needed to meet them as we were going to grab something to eat before we started drinking, so I needed to do that before I could start properly getting ready. I was a lightweight so needed to line my stomach. Then all my other friends turned up and none of our rooms were together, even though I had requested it, but not a lot we could do about it now. We lost track of time as we were chatting and ordered food at the hotel bar, but I could barely eat it, although I knew needed to so I wouldn't get pissed too quickly later. We had all forgotten to bring alcohol to drink whilst we got ready. I'd left mine on the side at home. My best friend had left hers chilling in the fridge, again at home. We ended up buying a bottle of prosecco at the hotel for £25, which was the price of five bottles in the supermarket, but we didn't have another option, really: as the time to get ready was dwindling away. It was all a rush yet again why does this always happen I will never learn and at this rate I was going to be late for my own hen do. Hopefully nothing else would go wrong, but let's face it, this was me.

I was ready in my nude coloured bodycon dress with bride to be sash and wedding veil covered in shamrocks and green diamantes, with a learner plate safety pinned to the back that Chynna had made and a St Patrick's day shot glass around my neck. I looked very tacky, just how I had always imagined. It was perfect and we were even on schedule. Everyone piled into my room drinks in hand and Chynna holding a three-foot inflatable penis.

We decided to take obligatory photos for social media and had a drink whilst finishing up, Debbie went outside for a fag and I knew when I heard OMG when the door opened that something was bad although she did like to over dramatize things. I looked out and it was actually worse than I thought. The weather warning had come true: it was snowing heavily now not a light dusting any more. I couldn't believe the amount of snow for such a short amount of time as we had only come back to the room an hour ago.

It did look pretty glistening in the moonlight, but was not practical in one's heels; one of us would end up breaking our neck. I ended up being late in the end as cabs were few and far between, so I was late for my own hen do. Despite the weather I had a great night regardless, got pissed quickly, didn't slip over in the snow and managed to make the toilet to be sick, so all in all a good night. The hangover the next day was one of the worst I had ever had even worse than the most recent one after the girlie meal. I am usually bad anyway since getting older. When I was in my early twenties, I would go out all the time and still get up for work and apart from feeling a bit tired, was fine. Nowadays I crawled out of bed, usually to the toilet, where I spent most of my day being sick and lying on the cold bathroom floor tiles. Then around nine p.m. I'd start to feel better. That day I don't even know how I got up and made it to breakfast. My sister and friends had all been to the spa already that morning and were sitting there tucking into a full English breakfast with mountains of toast. I couldn't even face a drink, let alone food, but managed to force down a grapefruit segment and then rested my head on the table whilst the others finished. I was rough.

Last Minute Wedding Crap

From being a little girl, I always knew that the fourth finger on the left hand was where you wore a wedding ring. I can't remember how I knew. My mum must have told me or I picked it up from TV or films, who knew. My innocent young self-thought that if you were wearing a ring you must be very happy with the person you were with as you were married and had found your soul mate and you lived happily ever after.

As I got older I realised that marriage was not perfect. My mum and dad were married and now divorced, and so many school friends' parents had separated. It just seemed the norm. This was around the millennium when divorce rates were very high and they had actually got better since. When I started going out clubbing, in my day that's what it was called, you could always spot a married man. That would be the first thing I would look at, even before their face, and found that men, even with rings on their finger, they would still try and chat you up. Not trustworthy at all. But it was only reading an article recently that I found out that the Romans believed that the vein in the ring finger ran directly to your heart. Who knew? I can't believe I had never asked why this was the case before. I just accepted it as this was the way it was. It got me to thinking about other things in my life that I had just accepted but never knew why.

I also found out that the reason you wear your wedding ring underneath your engagement ring traditionally is because it is closer to your heart.

I always had an image in mind of what wedding ring I would like, something glitzy; diamonds or cubic zirconia, I didn't mind. What I did know is I didn't want a straight band, as the diamond on my engagement ring was a cluster of diamonds that looked like a flower, so I didn't think it would sit right. Edward knew what he wanted too, palladium. I'd never heard of it, it sounded to me like something made up or like kryptonite, but when he showed me it just looked silver.

We decided to go along to some jewellers and try a few on. We didn't really have a budget as such but ones I had seen online were about two hundred pounds, so I was thinking for the two about five hundred pounds. So, two hours later, we were over a grand lighter and I had lost my engagement ring. Advice to anyone going wedding ring shopping, make sure you clean your engagement ring first as it looks disgusting up against bright shiny new rings, so much so mine was cleaned in the shop, but still needed recoating. Who knew that every eighteen months to two years you should get your ring recoated? I didn't so that had been sent off too. I felt lost without it. Kept checking my finger and panicking and then I remembered they also said that the best thing to do is start wearing it again after I got married, so they would both wear the same. So, ladies and gents, I am single for the next few weeks, lol. Six weeks to go and counting.

Now before when I originally brought my wedding dress, I thought I would be able to easily sell it if needed, but again the reality hasn't been as straight forward. I have taken lots of photos of the dress, but none do the dress justice. I had put it on a few online selling sites, but no one has even messaged me about it. I have even put it on there for a cheap price, I thought. Not only that, I have to get a new dress to wear to my Vegas wedding. I ordered a couple of dresses online, but both turned up and looked disgusting.

The first one was petite but long, made of lace and nude in colour, with load of sequins sewn into it; beautiful but not so nice on. Not only was it too big—and it was a size ten, I actually jumped for joy—it just didn't sit right. The back had a zip and instead of sitting flat it was all bumpy and looked like I had huge lumps coming out of my back and it was so long—and it was supposed to be petite—I would have still needed it taken up, even with heels.

The second dress was different, and I ordered an eight. I figured well, if the last dress, a ten was too big, I would aim for something smaller. But this was too small. It was lace again, white, strapless with a fishtail, but shorter in the front, but the boob parts were tiny. There was no way my boobs were going to fit in there.

I had rather large breasts and I hated them. Clothes just didn't look nice on me. I always had to wear a bra. I didn't wear low cut tops as think people would think I was some kind of slut, getting my tits out, whereas if someone flat chested wore the same top, no one would say anything. I had thought about having a reduction but just never done it I would have loved for my boobs to be the same size too. My right one was a lot bigger, so wearing no bra for me was not an option. I think I just kept this out of my mind when ordering dresses, hoping that they would be gone.

Well, third time lucky. I have ordered another one; hopefully this will look nice. The problem is, until I have the dress, it's hard to order accessories and shoes. You may be thinking why I don't just go and try dresses on like a normal person in shops.

Third time lucky dress was better but it turned up blue and I was sure I ordered white. It was pretty still and ninety percent better than the other two and had a built-in bra. It was lace again, but long with a slight train to it. It looked stunning on the model, but then they always do, don't they? You wouldn't order it if there was a picture of me wearing it, but that was the problem. I had been going for dresses that would not suit a short person. Another problem, I couldn't do it up myself. Would I have to call room service in the hotel, ask the waiter to do my dress up on my wedding day? Was that weird? It was also figure hugging and it actually made me look like I had a nice shape, but because it was a tad tight I thought it would be a bugger going for a wee and also, although I ordered petite, the train dragged on the floor, so I thought it may get filthy walking around Vegas and could have all sorts of stuff stuck to it. It was not like we are getting married and staying in the same venue all day. We were getting married in Vegas. We had booked the venue with a seven-minute ceremony and then were going to have dinner in their restaurant, but then who knows what we would do after. We would see.

I was now beginning to panic as with only three weeks to go I still had no dress, which meant no accessories. Edward said he would help and picked out some dresses that I thought were gross to be honest, but all the ones I had liked previously had looked shit, so what was the worst that could happen. Plus, these were way cheaper as they were not wedding dresses, they were just white dresses. Surprisingly I actually quite liked both of them when they arrived, but there was something about one of them. It was Bardot style with a skater skirt which was knee length on front and longer in the back. I had no make-up on when I tried it and I actually felt prettier. This was the one. It was ivory.

Now I had my dress—it wasn't how I imagined it at all, but it suited me and wasn't too much for Vegas, it was just right—now next stop was shoes and a bag. I had decided when we were getting married in this country to not wear a veil. Instead I wanted to wear a beautiful silver jewelled tikka hair chain. I didn't know if I still wanted to wear this in Vegas, but I already had it so I thought that I would take it with me, so I had options, I would order a veil too, so on the day I could see what I would prefer. This was the only problem with going away on your own: no one to tell you how you looked. I did say to my mum that I would Facetime her or video options, so she could tell me, so I could get her opinion, so thought I would just take everything.

Jewellery was the other thing, I don't really wear any other than my engagement ring, but would I need to wear anything on the day? Again, I would just have to take it just in case.

April

Malcolm picked up an old local paper and sat there staring at the announcements page.

'India Halberd and Edward James of Ipswich, Suffolk announce their engagement'

There was a picture of his daughter, who he hadn't seen since she was a teenager. She looked happy in the photo. He picked up a beer can and cracked it open. It was eleven a.m.

Later that day he called Marie in a state and needed to speak to her urgently. He still lived in the same house, but she was alarmed as she approached at how dilapidated it looked. She looked down the road and pictured India riding her bike and with her friends, happier times. The blossom trees that lined the road had gone and instead it was dark and dirty looking, not like when she had lived there.

As he opened the door she gasped as she was surprised at how much he had aged. He had thick lines running through his forehead and had barely any hair. She probably wouldn't have recognised him if he had walked past her in the street as he had lost so much weight. She hugged him, as he looked like he needed it, and as she walked into the front room the state of it shocked her. Empty beer cans and takeaway boxes covered the coffee table and the smell of smoke lingered in the air. She opened a window.

'When was the last time you got some fresh air? I must say you look awful.'

Malcolm half smiled but seemed in pain as he groaned at the same time. 'Nice to see you too, Mar'

He always used to call her that even though she hated it, but it still made her smile; she saw the glimmer in his eye that once was.

Not wanting to sit on the sofa she perched on the radiator.

'I want to see India,' he said

They had made an agreement after she realised Malcolm was India's father that they would never tell their daughter the truth. She didn't want her to know that she was the result of a drunken fumble in the back of a van. She already had a dad. She did have a dad, not biological, but she had the perfect little family, but when India was nine months old she realised that Ken may not be her father. She thought once she told Malcolm that India was his that he would step up, but he didn't want anything to do with her at first. It wasn't until she was seven Malcolm would drive down to the seaside to see her and they agreed that they would never tell her. Ken only found out when he confronted her about having an affair, and that's when they divorced.

'I don't care. I'm dying, Marie. I want to see her before it's too late'

Marie rolled her eyes. She had heard it all before and he was clearly pissed.

'No, for real. I only have a few months left if I am lucky and I want to see India before I die.'

Feeling bad, she looked into his brown sunken eyes and could see he wasn't lying; he looked ill.

'It's cancer, stage four, nothing more they can do for me.'

'I need a drink,' Marie said

'You still a Bacardi girl?'

'No, more gin now, but whatever you have got.'

He pulled out a bottle of Bacardi like it had been sitting in the cupboard waiting for her to come round. They sat and drank and reminisced about the old days when he would come into the office. He was drunker than he should have been and had started slurring his words.

'Do you remember that night when India was conceived.?'

'Yeah, of course I do,' she lied. She had flashbacks but nothing clear.

'You were out of it but well up for it,' he said. You had been gagging for it for weeks. So I saw my chance to satisfy your needs.'

'You're not seeing India.'

'You try and stop me,' he said, laughing.

'We agreed, we wouldn't tell her. India and I are finally talking again after I told her you was her father. Me bringing this up will fuck it all up again. I am not doing that to her again especially when she has her wedding in a couple of weeks. This should be a happy time. She knows now that you are her father so let's leave it up to her.'

'I don't care, Mar. I'm dying. I want to see her before it's too late. I've left everything in my will to her. She will inherit everything.'

Marie was about to leave as he wasn't getting the message. He grabbed her arm tightly so she couldn't move. 'Please, I need to tell her how sorry I am.'

'Get off me, you are hurting me,' she replied.

'No, not until you agree to speak to her.'

'You will be waiting a long time, Malcolm'

He then grabbed her other arm and started shaking her. 'You do not understand, Marie. I will see her one way or another.'

The look in his eyes scared her. She had only ever seen this look once before, then the night of her Christmas party in 1983 came flashing back to her. She had images of her being pushed down onto the floor of his dirty van while trying to turn her head, when he was trying to force himself on her. She tried to push him off as she kept saying it was wrong, she didn't want it to happen like this, but he kept on going, pulling her knickers off and ramming his hard penis inside her until she passed out. She never said no, but didn't consent either. Was it rape?

Two Weeks Before the Wedding

Turning on the television, not because I wanted to watch anything, I just wanted it on as background noise really, I just sat and scrolled through social media on my phone. Always the same pictures of people's dinners or children. Someone moaning or telling you where they were at that precise moment great for a burglar I thought. So boring. I did wonder why I kept my account open, but it did have its uses and you did get to be nosy and spy on people too. Plus, what else would I use my phone for, just texting and calling? Back to the days of my Nokia 3210 when all you could do was play snake. My eyes were quickly torn away from a photo of someone's breakfast of yet another avocado and egg on toast, when the news on in the background was talking about a murder in my local town where I grew up. I froze, dropping my phone, and did not even check to see if the screen was smashed. I walked closer to my fifty-inch television screen on the wall and the flashing images started to blur into my art deco inspired wallpaper as my eyes filled with water.

"Officers were called to Blackburn Road at nine p.m. yesterday evening where a man in his sixties was found brutally murdered in his property. Police are appealing for witnesses." the newsreader said.

Grabbing the remote, I turned the volume up to make sure I did not miss anything. Photographs appeared on the screen and the road I used to live on as a child popped up. The camera then panned to a house surrounded by police tape and a policeman and women hovering outside, trying to look busy. I recognised the red door with its brass lion knocker, a little different to how it was twenty-five years before. The front garden, once gravelled and kept neat with terracotta plant pots filled with pansies, had been replaced with stinging nettles and overgrown weeds nearly as high as the bay window. The net curtains, once a brilliant bright white and all the rage, now grey and torn. I knew exactly who lived there: it was Malcolm.

As I closed my eyes, tears ran down my cheeks. I went back to being a child again and could feel his filthy callused hands all over me and smell his coffee breath on my neck when he used to sneak up behind me. He had the roughest hands that had ever touched my skin, could tell he was in the building trade and never heard of hand cream. Memories came flooding back to me like a thunderstorm.

I thought back to how lively the road once was, children playing together happily on their roller skates or bikes. Neighbours chatting to each other from their front gardens and saying hello to passers-by; a lot more community spirit back then.

I knew now that he would never pay for what he had done and wished I could go back and tell the police what really happened.

Do not get me wrong, I was glad he was dead. I did have a mental kill list and he was at the top. If I had just told the police the truth when they had called me in for questioning back when I was thirteen, he would have paid for his crimes, but instead I didn't I just sat there and lied. But that was only because I was worried what it would do to my mum and she had lied to me for thirty plus years.

I needed Edward, but he had been away the last few days on a training course. I had tried calling him, but his number kept going straight to voicemail. Always seemed to be bloody unavailable lately when I needed him. He would say no signal or low battery when I questioned him. Malcolm was dead.

So, it was a week before the wedding. Most women would be working out every day, eating healthily, exfoliating and having face masks and having a cheeky couple of sunbeds to top up the tan but no, not me. I was at A& E again, this had been a regular place over the last few years surprised I didn't have my own parking space. The pain I was in today was excruciating. But I think stress was a contributing factor. I needed something stronger than the normal prescribed painkillers I had been taking. It took the doctor 8 attempts to put a canula in my arm before he gave up and asked a phlebotomist which really, I wish he had done after the second time he failed as now my arms were bleeding and holey great for wedding pics if there would even be a wedding now. My veins were hiding apparently. Morphine was finally flushed through with an anti-sickness medication and after that the wedding was out of my mind all I can remember was my black fluffy cardigan flying through the air Edward said I was hilarious totally off my head.

Luckily, I was only in for one night as other than giving me a hysterectomy which they wouldn't do as I was too young and hadn't had any children. There was nothing they could do other than manage my pain which I could do at home now with the stronger stuff I had been given. I even said to Edward I would understand if he didn't want to marry me now. I would totally understand if he did want to postpone the wedding as I wouldn't want to marry me at this present time. But, of course, he was amazing and said I was being silly. He loved me and wanted to marry me regardless, in sickness and in health.

I had so much planned to do before we left. Not only bridal maintenance, I still had to sort out clothes to take, packing, meeting up with family, but it all had to be put on hold now. Would we even be able to still go? At that moment I could barely walk. How was I going to go to another country where lots of walking would be involved? I couldn't expect Edward to push me around in a wheelchair, it wasn't fair. A & E as usual was a waste of time. I had been referred back to the GP, but the problem was if they then referred me to a specialist department, this could take months.

But I did what they said, went back the following day. I was given some tablets to try to help with pain, so hopefully these would kick in, in time. I was starting to stress now as you can imagine. Probably the stress of finding out Malcolm or Daddy dearest had been murdered. Not only was it less than a week to go, I was literally bed bound, I couldn't work I could barely get up to go to the toilet. Me and Edward spoke about whether we should cancel the wedding again. Of course, we didn't want to, but it may be our only option. What sort of time would we have away if I was laid up in bed the whole time? Not only that, this would be no fun for Edward as he would have to do the exploring on his own. I know everyone has problems, but I just felt at that moment we were so unlucky. How could this happen one week before the wedding? I was already worried. Rest was the best thing to do for now. We decided to make a firm decision two days before we were due to leave and see how I felt then. It was going to be a long week.

It was now Monday. We were due to leave on Wednesday and I was finally feeling better. Not fully recovered, but I could walk at least and my pain was nowhere near as bad as it had been. All systems were go. All the stress I had been under was not going to ruin my wedding, a breakaway was definitely what I needed.

Away from Malcolm, Spence and everything else I had been dealing with lately.

Now for bridal prep. A couple of weeks ago I thought the worst thing in the world was Edward's wedding present not arriving and my eyelash lady being off sick so she had to cancel my appointment. These were tiny things that didn't matter in comparison with what had happened. But now, whatever I could get done I would, so on the Tuesday I had booked to have nails, waxing and eyelashes done by someone else and my hair done, so other than packing I was pretty much ready to go. I had finally started to grow out my hair. When I imagined my wedding day, I would always have long flowing locks half up half down. After what happened with Malcolm when I was younger, I cut off my long hair into a bob and it had been that way ever since. I thought by cutting my hair I would be less girlie and attractive somehow.

Nine hours into a ten and a half hour flight I looked out of the window and could see snow. This was weird, but we were going over Canada according to the flight map on the TV.

All my earlier worries had left me as soon as we departed from Heathrow. Usually, I didn't like looking out if the window just in case I saw the wing on fire but the scenery was beautiful. We then flew over the desert and it was breath-taking, ripples of tanned coloured sand dunes, not a house in sight, just miles and miles of sand with the occasional lake or river running through.

We knew we were getting closer when we started to see buildings and houses and then all of a sudden, before we knew it, we were there. We had landed at McCarran International Airport. We could see the Vegas strip from the plane, just like I had imagined it, but a lot smaller; it looked no length at all. It was right in front of me looking like it was in touching distance.

Now before I came to Las Vegas I had done no research other than found out what things there were to do there, and, in my head, I actually thought Vegas would be a strip of hotels in a line surrounded by desert. I didn't realise that there would be houses. I thought it was a place that people came to on holiday. I forgot that people had to work there; they wouldn't fly in every day, what a donut. So, to see houses surrounding the strip surprised me.

I had only ever seen Vegas on films before, so it was surreal to be there. As soon as I stepped off the plane the heat hit me like opening an oven door and it was amazing on the transfer from the airport to the hotel. I was just in awe of the beautiful hotels and expensive cars and how clean it was. The sun was so hot, and I was also surprised at the amount of greenery around. Grass and palm trees lined the roads. I was also shocked by some of the billboards and number plates. Here it would seem you could have food names on your number plate, who knew, and the billboards would be promoting legal cannabis dispensaries. It was unreal.

We arrived at our hotel and it was gorgeous. We checked in got our room keycard. We were staying on the twenty-fifth floor out of twenty-eight so were quite high up. I couldn't see us taking the stairs at all; it would probably take us a week to get back down again. I thought the entrance to the hotel we had booked to have our wedding in originally was grand, but this was on another level. There was a huge gold water fountain in the lobby with beautiful high ceilings painted with murals, Italian architecture with polished marble floors that seemed to go on for days. I had never been to Italy, but I imagined this was how buildings would be there in the renaissance period. It was so clean too. I couldn't wait to see the room.

We had to walk through the casino to get to our room, very clever ploy to get you to gamble as soon as you arrived, but I was shocked to find that gamblers were smoking. As I pressed the key card to the door and saw the light turn green, I was excited. The hallway leading up to the room was fancy with plush navy and cream carpet and decadent wallpaper. I stepped into the room and couldn't believe my eyes. This was not your usual standard room; this was a suite. The nicest room I had ever stayed in. The bathroom was bigger than my front room and had a separate shower and bath and even had a separate toilet with a phone in there. I didn't think I would want to talk on the phone while doing my business, but it was good for emergencies like running out of loo roll, I suppose. There were twin sinks too and a TV, a dressing table and the decoration was a continuation of the lobby, very Italian. There were floor to ceiling mirrors everywhere, so good if you wanted to see how an outfit looked in full length, but not good if you hated looking in the mirror like me. Coming out of the bathroom, you came in to the bedroom: king-size bed, a massive flat screen and a walk-in wardrobe which automatically lit up when you opened the door, perfect. Then a few steps down from the bedroom was the sitting room, with a double sofa and two armchairs, a desk which was right by the window, so you could look out and see the fantastic view and, of course, another large flat screen TV. This was luxury, the nicest hotel I had ever set foot in.

Everything seemed to be going so well. There had been a few hiccups before we left like me being ill again, Edward's wedding present not turning up in time, but things were starting to look up. I had finally started to feel better; maybe the sunshine had helped. I turned on the TV in the room to see a picture of our wedding venue on there. Wow, it looked so nice, much better than in the photos. I was thrilled we were getting married there, something a bit different than what people usually expected for a Vegas wedding. I skipped from one room to the next, beaming about tomorrow and sent Spence, Jodie and my family the video I took as I entered the suite.

The uber picked us up from the hotel as it was about an hour's walk away to the marriage licence bureau and as soon as we pulled out onto the main road I could just see the very tall tower in the distance. As we got nearer it seemed to get further away, but we actually had to stop near on directly in front of it due to a red light, so we could see it in all its splendour. It was the perfect place to get wed. I looked up; it seemed to be higher than the clouds and I could see a viewing platform. Can you imagine getting married in the clouds, with the view of the Vegas strip or the desert behind you?

Licence got, that was easy. Edward had done what he needed to do online beforehand but was only in there two minutes, no queue or anything. It was a bit like a bank really, cashiers sitting behind desks a glass front protecting them. One security man sitting on the door.

One thing done, we decided to investigate our ceremony venue. It was amazing. We went up to the highest point and the sun was beaming down on us. The views were fair better than imagined. The only problem was is was quite windy up there, but we were hundreds of feet up. It was also a very public place; there were loads of other tourists around, not the private ceremony I'd anticipated, but didn't have time to change it now. This time tomorrow I would be a married woman, I thought. Now I was excited. An early night before the big day was very much needed as tomorrow, I would be Edward's wife.

The Big Day

I could not sleep. I must have got two hours at most, not because of nerves, because of jet lag. We didn't think that through with only arriving the day before. My eyes were so puffy I looked like I had been crying for a week. But miraculously I had no spots and not a cold sore in sight. This had been playing on my mind a lot. When I was little you could guarantee that school photo day I would have a cold sore. It was like my body knew, so I thought sod's law I would have some imperfection on my face. The only thing I had was puffy eyes, but I had a few hours before getting ready and there was an ice machine up the corridor so that could be plan B if they didn't go down before then. I did have a massive bruise on my left arm, though from the canula I'd had in the week before. Typical, although things could be worse; I could have been too ill to travel. I had to thank my lucky stars that it was only a bruise and puffy eyes I had to worry about.

It was weird how this day has been playing on my mind ever since I got engaged. But on the day of course, it didn't go to plan at all. I had given myself a couple of hours to get ready, which I thought was more than enough time as it didn't take me that long usually to get ready for special occasions etcetera.

My first error was that I hadn't practiced my make up, but I had a few photos of how I wanted it on my phone. I thought I would do my hair first then make up, as I was curling my hair, so I thought I would give it chance to drop. The prosecco was flowing nicely. I had been sticking ice on my eyes on and off for the last hour to try and reduce puffiness but it didn't help so I thought fuck it, there was nothing I could do now, I would just have to apply the makeup.

I started by cleansing my face, something I always do anyway, and moisturised. I have used the same moisturiser religiously since I was sixteen the same one my nan uses still. I then put on a makeup primer, the first time I had ever used one, then started with concealer, followed by a light foundation. My face had doubled in size at this point anyway due to the number of products on my face and I could feel my skin screaming at me, but I carried on. I had always wanted to contour so thought why not, my wedding day was a good day to do it.

I was wrong. I followed a guide I had found online for my face shape, which was very round, kind of looked like a Malteser shape, and started putting lighter concealer under my eyes in a triangle shape, on my chin, a waterfall type shape on my forehead and a bit on my cupids bow. I then started with a darker shade and practically drew lines on my face. I looked in the mirror and resembled a tiger. If Edward had walked in at that second, I think the wedding would have been off as honestly, I had never looked so ridiculous, but I blended like it said.

Next was highlighter and blusher and then I went on to do my eyebrows and eyeshadow. Why didn't I practise this beforehand. Maybe if I hadn't been ill the week before, things would have been different. I never really wore much make up usually and wore foundation twice a year if that. Right all finished and I didn't look like me at all; what the hell was I thinking? The only good thing I got out of this, though, was using a damp sponge and brushes to apply concealer and foundation made it look so much more flawless than using your fingers. This was something I would continue to do in future, if I ever wore this much make up again.

Before this day, I had planned to have loads of time to get ready, I thought I would Facetime or video call my mum and show her what I looked like, but the time literally went by in a flash. All I had time for was to take a few pics, but no videos, and obviously after what had happened with Mum, our relationship wasn't that great still, although I did feel bad as she'd told me about the miscarriage before she fell pregnant with me. She wanted us to be one big happy family. She said she didn't even realise Malcolm could be the father until he came in the office when I was nine months old. She said it was the only time she'd had sex since the miscarriage and she couldn't remember she was so drunk. She said that Malcolm had brought in her underwear to her in a bag, which reminded me of the time when I had hidden my knickers in a bag.

I sent pics to the family chat and also sent some to Spence and Debbie, as they were the most honest. Spence didn't reply, hadn't even texted me today, which I thought was rude. I knew there was a time difference, they were eight hours ahead of us in Vegas and it was late but still, it was my wedding day.

Edward was chilling in one of the many bars downstairs in the hotel, watching the Masters with a beer whilst I was running around like a headless chicken. But at last, I was ready. I grabbed my bouquet that I had made myself for the original wedding in September out of fake flowers, sunflowers, roses and eucalyptus. I thought I'd packed it well in my suitcase but when I got it out it was as flat as a pancake, but luckily I managed to salvage it for the day. I should have tried to wear in my shoes a bit too; as soon as I slipped my feet into them my feet hurt and I knew they were going to rub. I couldn't find the plasters I had packed so thought I would go down to the shop in the lobby next to the bar where Edward was, as I had a short dress on and blood on my feet would not be a good look.

There was a knock at the door just as I had picked up my bouquet and bag.

'You've forgotten the rings haven't you' I said, expecting to see Edward standing there, but I was left open mouthed when stood in front of me was Spence.

'Surprise!' he said and made a motion like he had just made rabbit appear from a hat. Fingers wriggling arms outstretched like he had jazz hands.

'What the fuck you doing here?'

Seeing Spence standing in front of me an hour before I was due to get wed was a surprise to say the least. After I got over the shock, I hugged him and invited him into the room.

'How did you know what room we were in?' I said.

'Lucky guess.'

Then I remembered the video I had sent of us entering the suite must have shown the door number on it.

'You do know I am getting married soon.'

'I had to see you before it was too late. You look beautiful, by the way.'

'Thanks. What's so bloody important that you flew all the way to Vegas?'

'You India, you're the reason, please don't marry Edward. I have loved you ever since we first met, I'm sorry I have left it until now to tell you but I had too.'

He then grabbed my face and kissed me softly on my lips.

I pulled away immediately and slapped him around the face.

'What do you think your doing' I replied

'Okay, I suppose I deserved that, how well do you even know him? I know you have had your doubts.'

I did not need this now. Sure, I had doubts, but that was normal, wasn't it?

Why now when I was all dressed up ready to get wed? The worst timing ever. There was a point when I had dreamt about marrying him but now, I was with Edward.

I had to go and meet him otherwise there would not be a wedding at all. Did this mean something, what a dilemma to be in. I was running out of time.

'I can't do this now. I am going to get married.' Great timing Spence. Time seemed to stand still and I became frozen and could not move just stood and stared at Spence holding onto this moment like it was my last. Spence leant forward again aiming for my lips with his. Just before they were about to touch I paused staring into his eyes then turned my head kissed him on the cheek and said.

'Goodbye'.

As I ran down the hotel corridor Spence shouted. 'Wait, you have no idea what I have done for you, for us'

As I approached the lift, I dare not look back at Spence as I might have not got in.

Had he left Sarah for me, what had he done?

Going down the twenty-five floors in the lift seemed to drag and go on forever. It seemed to stop at every floor to let someone else on. I felt like I was suffocating; I just needed to get out. Was I doing the right thing? I was content with Edward was that enough? Would I always regret not seeing what could have happened with Spence?

As the lift door opened, I saw Edward standing at the bar in his three- piece navy suit I could finally breath again. When he saw me he smiled and my head became clearer all of a sudden. He made me feel beautiful without saying anything, just by the way he was looking at me.

'Let's get wed,' I said, trying to forget about Spence and practically dragging Edward out the door. I still was unsure if I was making the right decision. Just hope he didn't follow us to the venue.

Seven minutes it lasted, but it was the most amazing seven minutes of my life and ended with us becoming man and wife. We ended up being upgraded to a private platform so were even higher than before. Looking into Edward's eyes when we were pronounced man and wife, I felt my happiest. I could hear music playing in my head.

At that moment all my earlier doubts disappeared. Spence was a distant memory, although he was still here somewhere in Vegas. He must have been staying in our hotel because you couldn't get in the lift without your room key card. All that build up and it was over; now we had done it. The only people witnessing it were the minister and photographer. It was now one a.m. in the UK due to the time difference. The sun was beaming down on us. Strangers from the deck below were shouting congratulations, which was weird but nice at the same time. Just hoped they couldn't see up my dress. We posed for photographs, which I struggled with usually, but today I couldn't stop smiling. My veil blew off as it was very windy up there but luckily Edward caught it before it flew over the edge. We had our wedding meal there but didn't eat much as I felt so sick probably because we were up so high. So, we ended up back at our hotel and before heading up to the room Edward decided to try his luck playing roulette he put two hundred and fifty dollars on black. His luck may not have been with him then but one thing you could sort of guarantee on your wedding night was sex so his luck was definitely in there. We had to consummate of course otherwise the wedding would not be legit. I wonder how many married couples manage to have sexual intercourse on their wedding night? Most of the weddings I had attended the grooms have been absolutely shitfaced so can't see how they could possibly perform. Edward did not have this problem. As soon as the suite door closed he bent down and untied my shoes and ran his hand up my leg to remove my garter. I was overcome with desire I needed him inside me now, my vagina was literally throbbing for him. As he entered me I felt complete. I had missed him. As I came, and lay next to Edward all I could think about was Spence. I didn't want to think about him I shouldn't have been especially after sex with my husband. Seems so weird calling him that.

The funny thing is with social media nowadays people know what you're up to, especially if you post a lot of things online, so friends and family would have known that we were married as they probably would have seen the pictures. Plus most people knew the date anyway, but do you know what, hardly anyone messaged us to say congratulations. It was weird really as if we had got married in this country we would have invited them and we hadn't heard a peep. It goes back to my earlier chapter about the guest list; shows some people aren't worth it at all. The next thing we had to arrange was the reception but now I felt like I couldn't even be bothered to invite them.

The rest of the time in Vegas went by in a blur. We done so much whilst we were there and had the most amazing adventure. We gambled, because you have to, and of course, we lost. We saw the Bellagio fountains, the Grand Canyon and even got to see a couple of shows whilst we were there. The hotel was absolutely stunning. I had never been to Italy, but our hotel felt like we were there. It was also the cleanest place I had ever seen. Cleaners were even washing down the walls daily. It was like being in another world. I was so glad I was well enough to enjoy this time and I would never forgot it for the rest of my life.

Not like where we lived in Suffolk where bird shit covered the pavements and litter was strewn in the roads. More importantly, Edward got to enjoy life for once. Okay, so I wasn't well the whole time we were there, but we managed to work around it. There were still things that we had wanted to do before we went but didn't, but we said we would most definitely go back.

After we were married, we must have seen six other couples in wedding attire having pictures and wandering around Vegas. It seemed a bit surreal. I know it was a popular place to get married, hence why we got married there, but I didn't realise how much. You could even have a fake wedding here to fool your friends and family and you could hire suits and wedding dresses from the chapels if you wanted to. There were a lot of chapels exactly how you would imagine them to be, lit up, white with a steeple, with fake flowers in the windows and outside.

We landed in London; looking out of the window of the 747 the weather was dreary. It looked freezing, nothing like the glorious sunshine we had left. But we were married; I was a married woman, how scary. I instantly felt older. Also, it was so easy to get married there. I was happy and sad at the same time. This showed you how much things can change. In just eight months since writing this I was already married. Looking forward to the next chapter in our life. All the stress, heartache and planning could have been avoided if we had just decided to do this earlier.

If I could give any advice to anyone who's engaged and starting to plan a wedding, start by thinking about what you want first and foremost, not what you think everyone wants you to have or what's normal, because that doesn't apply any more. At the end of the day, it is one day; regardless of cost, guests, dress, the outcome is still the same. I ended up getting married in a cheap dress I bought online three weeks before the wedding and I had more compliments on the dress than I ever thought I'd get. Whether they tell you you're beautiful or not, just because they feel they have to, as long as the dress makes you feel pretty then that's all the matters. I worried so much in the end that I needed to be perfect for this one day, but life isn't perfect and nor am I, and my husband would have still married me even if I was in my dressing gown because he wanted to marry me. Not what I looked like on the outside, just how I was on the inside. I just wish I had realised this sooner.

So, the moral of this story is, it doesn't matter how much you spend on your wedding, or who is there, as long as you are there and your partner; it is all that matters. Whether you spend thousands or hundreds, the outcome is still the same; you are married to the person you love and at the end of the day behind closed doors it is just you two from now on. We had been on a rocky journey since the engagement. It had not been smooth sailing but that is life. It wasn't easy and everything we had been through had made us stronger for it. Seven minutes it took to become man and wife after all the planning, all the stress, and I wouldn't change a thing. Instead of having one full on day where it goes by in a flash and you are thousands lighter, we had five days where we had seen a different part of the world, somewhere we both wanted to go, and even had our honeymoon chucked in. Of course, it would have been nice to have family there to witness it but at the end of the day it was about two people, the bride and groom, and sometimes love makes you selfish.

I gave myself a year to change. First step was realising it wasn't my fault and I hadn't done anything to encourage them. I was a child when most of this happened. I finally went to the police, and telling them about the rape and the abuse I suffered for those two years at the hands of Malcolm McCormack, my dad, I finally feel like a weight had been lifted slightly off of my shoulders, as now I had told the truth. I even told my mum. I know he will never get to answer for his crimes unless they hold a séance, but I know what happened and it was not my fault, none of it.

Edward thought I was beautiful enough to marry so that was all that mattered now, our future together, starting a family. I couldn't wait for the next chapter in our life. In other good news, I found out I was pregnant and we were over the moon as I had been told by doctors in the past that it may not be possible for me to have children due to the endometriosis, so falling pregnant naturally was a miracle.

So, nine months to a baby coming soon.

One Month Later

As I opened the door the police were standing there.

Someone growing weed again probably down the road.

'May we speak with Mr Edward James? The policeman said' phew I thought nothing to do with me. Not that I had done anything wrong but I did start to panic thinking what if I had done something and didn't realise it.

'Come in,' I said, ushering them in. 'You want a drink or anything?' 'Edward,' I shouted out to him as he was in the garden, 'the police are here to see you'.

'No thank you, ma'am we are here on official police business.'

Oh I thought what could they possibly want Edward for? Maybe he had witnessed something and not told me.

Edward came in from the back garden holding a hammer.

'Edward James, put down the hammer, please, sir'

Edward did as he was told and dropped the hammer on the floor.

'Edward'? I asked him, confused.

'Where has that hammer come from?'

'Edward James, I am arresting you on suspicion of the murder of Malcolm McCormack'

They kept saying the lines that police say on the TV programmes I had watched, reading him his rights. It didn't seem real; this wasn't happening.

'What's going on? Edward wouldn't hurt anyone. You have got it wrong,' I shouted.

'I called them India, it's okay'
Edward looked into my eyes and smiled rubbing my tummy.

I looked down at the hammer laying on the carpet floor, stained with what looked like dried blood. Was that the hammer that had been used to bludgeon Malcolm's head in? I had heard rumours in the town that was how he was killed, but he couldn't have done it. He wasn't even in the same town. He was away training again at the time.

'The murder weapon is there.' He pointed to the bloody hammer. 'You will find all my fingerprints on it.'

It didn't make sense at all.

As he was marched out the front door in handcuffs he winked at me and mouthed, 'Nobody will ever know, I love you.'

Nobody will ever know what? I thought. Did he think I had murdered Malcolm, because I didn't as much as I had wanted to.

I gasped and it hit me, it was Spence.

The end.